The moment the idea of Gabe Knight stripping off her clothes and joining her on top of this table popped into her hazy thoughts, she knew she had to end the embrace.

"Gabe." She offered him one last breathless kiss, then pushed her fingers between their lips. "Gabe, we have to stop."

"I know." With a throaty growl, he pulled away, dropping little kisses to her fingertips as he retreated. "I know you're right. I don't like it. But you're right."

Despite the rumpled coal-dark hair and the collar she'd wrinkled with her eager hand, his deep blue eyes were as clear and focused as ever. "So why did you kiss me? And yes, I know, it was a team effort. But I'm interested in your motives."

Motives? She hadn't thought that far ahead. Still trying to regulate her own breathing, Olivia ran her fingers through her own hair, dismissing the probing question. "Don't analyze it, okay? Just accept the thank-you."

"That was more than a thank-you."

KANSAS CITY COVER-UP

USA TODAY Bestselling Author

JULIE MILLER

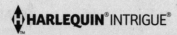

HARLEQUIN® INTRIGUE®

I wanted to take a moment to remind readers that my Precinct books, while
set in a real place, are works of fiction. Kansas City is a safe, welcoming
place to visit—full of history, art, music, theater, beautiful fountains, fun
activities, great sports, fabulous places to shop, yummy barbecue and
some of the friendliest people in the country.

With thanks to my family and friends in Kansas City.
Thanks, too, to the police, fire and rescue, city engineers and other
public servants who serve KC and the surrounding metropolitan area.

My stories may be fiction, but Kansas City is real and wonderful—
a great city to live in or visit.

Hope to see you there!

ISBN-13: 978-0-373-69826-4

Kansas City Cover-Up

Copyright © 2015 by Julie Miller

Recycling programs
for this product may
not exist in your area.

Printed in U.S.A.

www.Harlequin.com

Julie Miller is an award-winning *USA TODAY* bestselling author of breathtaking romantic suspense—with a National Readers' Choice Award and a Daphne du Maurier Award, among other prizes. She has also earned an *RT Book Reviews* Career Achievement Award. For a complete list of her books, monthly newsletter and more, go to juliemiller.org.

Books by Julie Miller

HARLEQUIN INTRIGUE

The Precinct: Cold Case Series
Kansas City Cover-Up

The Precinct Series
Beauty and the Badge
Takedown
KCPD Protector
Crossfire Christmas

The Precinct: Task Force Series
The Marine Next Door
Kansas City Cowboy
Tactical Advantage
Assumed Identity
Task Force Bride
Yuletide Protector

Visit the Author Profile page at
Harlequin.com for more titles

CAST OF CHARACTERS

Gabriel Knight—This veteran crime reporter has no love for KCPD since they've never been able to solve his fiancée's murder. Determined to find justice, he insinuates himself into the department's latest murder investigation, certain the two deaths are connected. But working with Olivia Watson has dangerous, unexpected consequences.

Detective Olivia Watson—After a disastrous relationship that broke her heart and nearly derailed her career, Olivia trusts no man. This third-generation cop and cold-case investigator is certain that pairing her with Gabe Knight to solve a six-year-old murder is a mistake.

Danielle Reese—This fledgling reporter was about to break a career-making story when she was murdered six years ago. What secrets died with her? And how far will her killer go to keep the truth buried?

Leland Asher—His ruthless business practices and suspicious influence over local politicians have made him a wealthy man—and a prime suspect in a number of crimes. He's either innocent, or really good at getting away with murder.

Ron Kober—Was he ready to spill the truth about his former boss?

Elaine Kober—Ron's wife. She helped make him a success. How far will she go to protect her marriage and her money?

Misty Harbison—Ron Kober's executive assistant. She's a young, pretty blonde.

Stephen March—What is his fascination with Olivia?

Detective Marcus Brower—Olivia's former partner.

Jim Parker, Max Krolikowski, Trent Dixon, Katie Rinaldi and Lieutenant Ginny Rafferty-Taylor—Olivia's Cold Case Squad team.

The Host—A mysterious benefactor? Or an unknown threat?

Chapter One

"How is this a cold case?" Detective Olivia Watson squatted down beside the body with the bashed-in head lying on the plush office carpet.

The pool of blood looked fresh enough. The alleged murder weapon, a civic volunteerism trophy from the dead man's own desk, had already been bagged and packed away by the CSI trading notes with the medical examiner nearby. A uniformed officer and two building security guards were holding back a bevy of shocked and grieving office staff from the Kober & Associates PR firm, as well as curious onlookers from other businesses in the building beyond the yellow crime scene tape that blocked off the victim's outer office door. The two Kansas City PD detectives on the far side of the room interviewing the distraught secretary who'd discovered her boss's body after her half-day spa appointment seemed to have the crime scene well under control. So why call in representatives from the Fourth Precinct's Cold Case Squad?

Olivia rested her forearms on the thighs of her dark wash jeans and studied the sixtyish man's still features again. The glass-and-steel high-rise in downtown Kansas City was almost as new as the murder itself. She was used to working cases with pictures out of dusty boxes and autopsy reports that raised a lot of unanswered questions. She'd worked with skeletal remains and mummified corpses and alleged victims whose bodies had never been found at all. Most people assumed the Cold Case Squad was an easier gig than working a fresh investigation. She liked to think of it as a *smarter* assignment, requiring more insight and diligence than other divisions at KCPD.

Olivia was a third generation cop, like two of her three brothers. And the third one worked in the medical examiner's office. After two years in a uniform, five years in vice and the past year working cold cases, she'd learned that killers who'd eluded capture and thought they'd gotten away with murder often proved to be more devious and more dangerous than any other criminal out there. It was her job to track down those killers and finally get justice for those forgotten victims whose memory often died with their closest family and friends.

So why was she here to assist two perfectly capable detectives when there was a stack of her own investigations back at HQ to sort through?

"There must be a connection to one of our dead file cases. But if there is, I don't see it yet." She glanced up at her new partner, Jim Parker—back from the dead himself after a particularly harrowing undercover assignment for the Missouri Bureau of Investigation. "Do you?"

Jim's green eyes surveyed the room the way she had. "I recognize Ron Kober from the newspapers. Besides owning a Top 50 company here in KC, he helped get Adrian McCoy elected to the State Senate a few years back. Looks like he was doing pretty well on his own, without the senator."

Olivia arched a dark eyebrow. "Until today."

She liked Jim well enough, respected his reputation as a cop, appreciated that he got her sarcastic sense of humor. But after that humiliating debacle with her last partner, learning to trust him was hard. Thankfully, Jim was a newlywed, completely crazy about his wife, Natalie, and showed nothing but a friendly professional interest in his relationship with Olivia. Still, she found herself thinking about her words before she spoke to him, guarding her thoughts and feelings, which was no mean task for a woman with her volatile Irish roots.

"A man with this kind of money probably has plenty of enemies," Jim suggested.

An angle which she was sure the lead detectives were already exploring. Still didn't explain why she and Jim were here. She looked back down at the body, willing the corpse to speak and share his secrets. But she wasn't psychic and dead men didn't talk. However...

Her eyes went past Kober's body to a scrap of torn paper underneath the desk. She snapped a picture with her cell phone before reaching over the dead body to pick it up with the sterile gloves she wore.

Jim crouched down beside her. "What did you find?"

Olivia turned the tiny square over between her thumb and index finger. "Four numbers. I don't know. It may just be a piece of trash."

"Looks like a torn-up piece of stationery." Jim picked up the wastebasket beside the desk and set it between them to sort through its contents.

But there were no other little hand-torn shreds like this one. "Could be the last digits of a phone number."

Jim replaced the wastebasket and stood. "Or part of an address or social security number."

"Or a locker number or part of a combination lock." Olivia straightened beside him, spotting a pad of dove-gray paper on the desk that matched the piece in her hand. She picked it up and angled it in the light to see if she could read any indentations in the surface. But there were too many marks from previous notes to make out anything specific. "Maybe it's just a testament to their housekeeping service not doing its job, and isn't related to the crime at all."

Just in case, though, she jotted the 3620 in her notebook before handing the scrap of paper and Kober's scratch pad over to the CSI.

She tucked her own notepad into the pocket of her short leather jacket and peeled off her gloves, following Jim to the door. "So if this isn't our case, why are we here?"

Jim nodded to the detectives hovering over the weeping woman across the room. "Hendricks and Kincaid are taking lead on Kober's murder here. Sawyer Kincaid called us in as a courtesy."

Frowning, Olivia stuffed the gloves into the back pocket of her jeans. "And he didn't say why?"

"He just said it was a directive from higher up." He touched her shoulder to indicate he was taking a detour. "Looks like they're wrapping up that interview. I'll go ask if they can make sense of any of this yet."

While her golden-haired partner crossed the room, Olivia indicated she'd head on downstairs and meet him at the car.

She shouldn't have acknowledged the visceral impact of the short black hair and chiseled cheekbones of the man waiting just outside the office door as she passed him. Admitting any kind of gut-kick attraction to a man was, at least, an inconvenience, and, at most, a huge mistake. Her relationship with Marcus had taught her that.

But the man's piercing blue gaze locked on and followed her through the doorway. The skin at the nape beneath her short hair tingled with awareness at his interest. Only, she wasn't sure if it was sensual nerves fluttering to attention, or an alarm going off. Either way, she wasn't about to flutter for any man, and she wasn't going to ignore those survival instincts that warned her of danger.

Olivia stopped in the middle of the assistant's office and turned to face Mr. Tall Dark and Staring. "May I help you?"

He pulled back the front of his tan corduroy sport coat and tucked his hands into the pockets of his jeans, assuming a casual stance she wouldn't match. "I can tell you why you're here, Detective Watson."

Her chin jerked up ever so slightly at the stranger calling her by name. Un-uh. That wasn't an advantage she'd allow. Her hand instinctively came to rest over the Glock holstered to her belt. "Do I know you, Mister...?"

"Not really." The man straightened from the wall where he'd been leaning, and she could see he stood a good five or six inches over her five-foot-seven-inch height. "Ron Kober is the man my fiancée Danielle Reese was getting inside information from for a story she was writing when she was murdered six years ago."

"Danielle Reese?" Why did that name sound familiar? Didn't matter. This guy was still a couple steps ahead of her in the conversation, and she didn't like it. "You didn't answer my question. Who are you?"

"Gabriel Knight."

Was that supposed to mean something to her? That deep, succinct announcement made it sound as though he thought he was somebody important. But she'd have remembered a face like that. Not exactly handsome with all those sharp, unsmiling angles, but definitely interesting.

Olivia blinked, silently reprimanding herself for even noticing such irrelevance. It was more important to note that she saw no sign that he was wearing a gun, and since he hadn't flashed a badge to identify himself, he couldn't be a cop. Gabriel Knight must be a curiosity seeker who'd probably lied to the uniformed guard about having some kind of information on the case so he could get close enough to see the dead body.

"Sir, did one of the detectives ask you to come past the crime scene tape for questioning?" He didn't answer. Proof enough for her that Gabriel Knight was trespassing on the crime scene. She thumbed over her shoulder to the hallway. "Then you can't be in here."

"I've got press credentials." He tugged at the cord hanging around his neck and pulled a plastic card from his shirt pocket. "I'm covering the murder for the *Journal*."

A reporter? "Yeah, well my badge outranks your little piece of plastic. If you'll wait out front with the other reporters, the press liaison will be downstairs to give a briefing in a few minutes." She took him by the arm and turned to escort him into the hallway, but the man didn't budge.

"You need to talk to me." His voice was low and articulate, and, without being a breathy whisper, was for her ears alone. "I have information on this case. That's why the officer out front let me through."

"Then you should talk to Detective Kincaid or Detective Hendricks." She released him to point out the big man with the dark hair and the black man with the diamond stud in his left earlobe in the other room. "I can introduce you when they're through with their witness."

But Gabriel Knight grabbed her elbow and pulled her back beside him. "You may not read the paper, but

I know who you are, Detective Watson. You and your partner are part of the cold case team, working older, unsolved crimes. Like the murder of Dani Reese. She was an investigative reporter, a colleague of mine. The woman I loved. She was found dead at an abandoned warehouse down on the river docks six years ago. Shot through the head like some common criminal. I'm the one who called Chief Taylor and suggested he send a team from your department here this afternoon."

Olivia jerked her arm from his grasp.

"You called the Fourth Precinct chief?" Who'd filtered the request down through Sawyer Kincaid and on to Jim and her. She hated anyone who felt they were entitled enough to break the rules of standard police procedure whenever it suited them. She could do the low, threatening voice, too. "You know, we have real work to do, Mr. Knight. KCPD is not at your beck and call to dig up sidebars for whatever story you're working on."

"Trust me, Detective, there is nothing more real to me than finding Dani's killer. If your people won't do it, I will."

Her people? Cops? Like her friends and father and grandfather and brothers? The same men and women who'd solved her own mother's brutal slaying two decades earlier? This guy was bashing them?

And then something else he said registered, cooling the defensive anger that had flashed through her veins. *The woman I loved.*

She empathized with the kind of senseless violence, anger and grief Gabriel Knight had suffered more than he knew. It only took one deep breath, one thought of her mother's smiling face, to remember her sensitivity training. "Every victim believes the death of his or her loved one is our most important case. I'm sorry for your loss. But if the department hasn't made enough progress on Ms. Reese's death to suit you, it's only because there haven't been any substantial leads. Not because we've given up."

"*This* is a lead. There has to be a connection to Kober. Find it."

"I promise you, if we get new information on your fiancée's death, we'll look into it."

"Coming from you, that's not terribly reassuring."

Bristling at the dig that felt inexplicably personal, coming from a man she'd never met, Olivia gestured toward the yellow tape. She bit down on the urge to demand an explanation and invited him to walk beside her. "We never give up on a case. Ever. But some take longer to solve than others. It's a matter of prioritization. We review cases every day and try to focus our time, money and manpower where it can do the most good."

"You're preaching departmental protocol, Detective Watson. And that's not a good enough answer." He stopped at the outer door, dipping his head slightly as he faced her one more time. "You find out who killed Kober, and I guarantee you'll find a lead on Dani's murderer. It may even be the same man who committed both crimes."

With that warning, he ducked beneath the tape and stalked away. Olivia shook her head at the uniformed officer's questioning look about whether or not he needed to stop Knight before he pushed his way through the gathering of onlookers and got on the elevator.

She was still processing the oddly charged and cryptic encounter when she felt a tap at her elbow. She nodded to Jim and he lifted the crime scene tape for her to exit in front of him. "You know who you were talking to, don't you?"

"Yeah. He said his name was Gabriel Knight. He's a reporter."

"Not just any reporter." They stepped onto the elevator and Jim pushed the button for the ground floor. "Gabe Knight writes the Crime Beat column for the *Kansas City Journal*."

Her instincts about men must still be out of whack after dumping Marcus. Otherwise, she'd have pieced together the name with the clues he'd dropped.

"He's the guy who wrote all those editorials about KCPD not being able to catch the Rose Red Rapist?" And when the task force did finally catch the creep and put him on trial, there hadn't been one word of praise or apology, merely a recitation of facts and something like, *"About damn time."* Olivia groaned at her ineptitude as she walked out with Jim. Somehow she felt as if she'd betrayed her brethren cops by even having a conversation with the department's most outspoken critic. "And I was nice to him. Well, I was civil. He thinks Kober's murder is related to the unsolved death of his fiancée a few years back. Danielle Reese? He's the one who got us invited to the crime scene."

They circled the gathering of television cameras and reporters on their way to her SUV. She felt Knight's blue eyes following her from the crowd awaiting the press conference as they crossed the street, but studiously ignored the urge to meet his watchful gaze.

"He probably approached you because he thought you'd be softhearted and sympathetic to his cause." She glared at Jim over the hood of the car before they both climbed in. "Clearly, he doesn't know you very well."

Okay, so Jim's dry wit could make her laugh, too, just like her brothers' teasing guff usually did.

Olivia's smile faded as they fastened their seat belts.

"He's poking his nose into our crime scene, trying to get the scoop on the rest of the press—and then he turns around and criticizes us for not catching every last bad guy, or doing it fast enough to suit his idealistic time-table? That just sticks in my craw."

She looked through the windshield to glare at the presumptuous Mr. Knight. But those smug blue eyes were nowhere to be seen. Even with a second search among the reporters gathered in front of the building, she didn't spot his rich, coal-black hair. "That son of a…" Had that self-important buttinsky snuck back inside the building? Un-uh. Not on her watch.

Olivia pulled her keys from the ignition and opened her door. "Can you get a ride with somebody? I'm going to have a couple more words with Mr. Knight."

Jim climbed out on the opposite side. "Do you need me to go with you?"

"No, I can handle him." As soon as he'd closed his door, she hit the locks and hurried around the hood of the car.

"Olivia, we're a team, remember? I've got your back."

"I know."

"How come I don't quite believe you mean that?"

Olivia stopped midcharge. Marcus Brower had supposedly had her back, too. And while her former partner had never once let her down out on the streets, his betrayal behind closed doors would probably always taint her ability to trust a man who wasn't family again.

But Jim Parker didn't deserve to be blown off because some other guy was a two-timing jackass she'd put her career on hold for. "Sorry. You and I are still in the getting-to-know-you phase, I suppose. Sometimes, people like Gabriel Knight don't take a woman cop seriously. I need him to understand that when I tell him to go away and let us handle things, I mean it."

Seemingly satisfied with the apology and that much of an explanation, Jim nodded and pulled out his cell phone. "The man's a cool customer from what I hear. Don't let him rile that Irish blood of yours."

"Too late for that. Say, maybe you can pull out the file on Dani Reese's murder so I can get up to speed on whatever it is Knight is blaming us for. See if we can find that connection to Kober he claims, too." She waved goodbye as Jim placed his call. "I'll catch up with you back at HQ."

"Roger that." She heard an amused voice behind her as she darted across the street. "Good luck, Mr. Knight."

Chapter Two

"Are you deaf or stupid, Mr. Knight?" Gabe halted on the seventh floor's concrete landing at Olivia Watson's voice. "I'll bet it's neither one. You're just too damn arrogant to think that the rules apply to you, aren't you?"

It was the husky undertones coloring that voice, not the words themselves, that turned him to face the detective.

She glared at him from the bottom of the stairs, her chest subtly expanding and contracting beneath that trim leather jacket. It hadn't taken the police as long as he'd expected to notice him sneaking through to the back stairs and chase him up six flights of steel and concrete. This one was smart. Determined. Ticked off.

"Detective," was all the verbal acknowledgment he gave her. Because the hammer of his traitorous pulse was already acknowledging way more than it should, given that she was a cop, she was a Watson and she wanted to shut down his investigation.

The badge she wore like a necklace, the gun resting on the curve of her hip, and the accusation filling her green? gray? gold?—curiously indefinable eyes did little to diminish her striking beauty. She might wear her sable dark hair in that mannish cut and talk the same sarcasm and suspicion the male cops he knew used, but there was no mistaking the femininity in that husky voice and her leggy, athletic build—or his damnable reaction to them.

For the six years he'd been obsessed with finding Dani's killer, he'd been anything but a fan of KCPD. That another woman, a cop—Thomas Watson's daughter, no less—should get him thinking randy thoughts about stripping off all that hardware and attitude didn't sit real well with his celibate devotion to the fiancée he should have saved. His curious fascination with the mysteries surrounding the lady detective who'd tracked him down rankled his long-held contempt for the police department that had failed to bring Dani's killer to justice.

"I need you back downstairs," she ordered. "Now."

Thanks. The sharp command took the sexy out of her voice and made it easier for Gabe to dismiss his far too male reaction to her.

He moved to the edge of the landing, toward the woman attempting to stop his return to the taped-off office suite on the tenth floor. "There's no such thing as a perfect crime, Detective. Only an inability to see and understand the clues that are there. If you aren't willing to find the connection between the two murders, I will."

With a curt nod, he turned to the next set of steps, skipping a stair and another pointless conversation with KCPD.

"Don't make me pull my gun, Mr. Knight."

He stopped and leaned over the railing. "Why don't you join me and do some real police work, instead of standing there, trying to make me think you can stop me."

"Trying?" The curse that followed definitely wasn't feminine. Gabe laughed and climbed the steps. He heard her charging up the stairs after him.

Good. He'd goaded at least one KCPD cop into taking

some action. Even if she argued every step of the way, Detective Watson's presence would get him back into Ron Kober's office so he could pick up what the CSIs and detectives were saying, and he could get a closer look at the crime scene for himself.

But Gabe's smug smile flatlined when he felt a strong tug at his shoulders. "What the—"

"You are officially trespassing in a restricted area." Olivia yanked his jacket halfway down his arms, twisting them back and restricting his movement long enough to snap a pair of handcuffs around his wrists. She wrapped her hand around his elbow and turned him to face her. "And you're annoying the hell out of me. Now, either go out front with the other reporters, or I'll happily escort you to a jail cell myself."

Locking his hands behind his back wasn't going to stop his investigation. "I know Dani Reese is in your cold case files."

"Fine. I'll look it up when I get back to the precinct. You're still leaving."

With a tug on his arm and a dare to defy her challenge bringing out the green in her eyes, Gabe reluctantly fell into step beside her and headed back down the stairs. She might have changed his direction, but she hadn't silenced his voice. He calmly explained his reasons for ignoring her order to clear the building. Again. In case Olivia Watson had more bravado than brain cells going for her. "I'm trying to speed the process here, Detective. Dani was getting inside information on strong-arm tactics and a possible mob connection to Senator McCoy's campaign. Six years ago. And now he's running for re-election?"

"I get your timeline. And I get that the events are too serious to dismiss as coincidence. You said Kober was feeding your fiancée intel on the senator's campaign?" Her fingers tightened around his arm as they turned the corner—probably standard procedure to provide extra balance to a man in handcuffs. But his pulse leaped at Olivia's firm grasp on him, momentarily distracting him from the questions laced with skepticism. "How do you know that? Were you working the story, too?"

"No. It was Dani's big scoop. She was trying to make a name for herself. I didn't even realize what she was onto until it was too late." Taking a deep breath, he pushed aside his lusty reaction to Detective Watson's touch and let his heart fill with its customary guilt and grief. It wasn't hard to replace Detective Watson's changeable eye color with the sky blue beauty of Dani's soft gaze in his mind. "I started reading the notes she had saved on a zip drive one night. I found Kober and Senator McCoy's name, along with the draft of a story on kickbacks from Leland Asher."

Olivia's pace slowed. "The alleged crime boss?"

"You know there's nothing *alleged* about the way he conducts business. That man has more ways to launder money than an industrial linen service. When I confronted Dani about the scope of what she was working on—and warned her of the danger—she got mad and stormed out. By the time I found out where she was meeting her contact, it was too late." He stopped on the landing, needing to set his feet to withstand the memory that chilled his blood like a ghost passing through his body. He should have stopped Dani that night. He should have gone with her. He should have covered the damn story himself and not let a junior reporter—no matter how good her instincts might be—take that kind of risk. When he found his breath again, when he could firmly close the door on the gruesome images from the past, Gabe continued. "The next time I saw Dani, she was lying on a slab in the morgue. She'd been shot three times. The ME had to identify her by the dragon tattoo on her ankle and what was left of her teeth."

"I'm sorry." Olivia's fingers curled into a fist and she pulled away. "I know that's rough. Losing someone you love is tough enough. Seeing them in the morgue…"

Gabe glanced down to see her unfocused gaze staring off into the corner. Was that real empathy? Some haunting remembrance of another case she'd worked? An official training technique to gain his cooperation? Didn't matter.

"Save your pity. Do your job." As soon as he spoke, her gaze snapped back to his. "A couple of dock workers found Dani lying beside her abandoned car near an old warehouse. The killer had taken her engagement ring and billfold, and tried to make it look like a robbery. That's how KCPD investigated her death, as a carjacking gone bad. But I tell you, it was all about the story she was writing. That's why you people never solved the case."

"You people?" He watched her bristle at the dig against cops, against someone much closer to the case than she probably realized. Detective Watson wrapped her hand around his arm again and pulled him into step beside her. Ah, hell. She hadn't really been listening. She was just humoring him. "Less talking and more moving, okay, Knight?"

Gabe lengthened his stride to get ahead of her. He stopped on the next landing and turned, forcing her to halt on the step above him. He had no problem getting in her face and making his point. "Connect the dots, Olivia. If Ron Kober knew enough about Leland Asher's influence on the campaign to share it with the press six years ago, I don't imagine either Senator McCoy or Asher would want Kober around now. McCoy is already under investigation. If Kober told anyone what he knew? What Dani knew? You know how the press is ready to jump on any hint of a scandal during a campaign."

To her credit, she didn't back down from the confrontation. "Look, I understand why you think there could be a shared motive between the two deaths. I promise, I will read through your fiancée's case file. But I told you, I'm not even assigned to Kober's murder. All I can do is inform Detectives Hendricks and Kincaid that—" She stopped abruptly and angled her head to the side.

"I'm telling *you*."

She leaned toward the steel railing. "Shh."

He leaned with her, demanding she pay attention. "It makes sense that the same person who wanted Kober dead might also have wanted to silence Dani. The two murders—"

"Shut. Up." She pushed him back against the wall with a hand over his mouth.

And then he heard it, too. The double click of a door opening and closing. Footsteps in the stairwell below their position.

Running footsteps.

Even the pretense of listening to his outpouring of information had ended. She was in full cop mode now. Olivia pulled her hands from his chest and chin and plucked the radio off her belt. "This is Detective Watson. Has the building been cleared?" While other officers in the building responded, she pulled a ring of keys from her jeans and unlocked his cuffs. Her next question was to him. "Did you bring any of your reporter friends with you?"

Gabe shook his head. He shrugged his corduroy

jacket back onto his shoulders and zeroed in on the sounds of huffing breaths and hurrying footfalls below.

There was the punch of another door handle and a muttered curse before Olivia got back on the radio. "I've got activity in the south stairwell. Maybe somebody who shouldn't be here snuck in." Her gaze tilted up to his. Okay, so she could do the subtle dig thing, too. "Or our perp is trying to sneak out. I'll get eyes on it. Watson out." She pushed open the door marked with a three and pointed into the main building, dismissing him. "Can I trust you to find your way to the front door all by yourself?"

She must have accepted his silence as an agreement because she put away her handcuffs and radio and pulled her gun in the same fluid movement. Then those long legs were booking it down the stairs.

OLIVIA PUSHED ASIDE the charged energy that hummed through her system after trading words with Gabe Knight and focused on her pursuit of the unknown subject. She saw the second-floor door swinging shut and pressed her back against the concrete block wall, keeping her attention on both the door and the stairs, uncertain which way the intruder had gone until she heard the deep, ragged panting of a man trying to catch his breath from a location below her. He'd heard her coming and had ducked into a corner to hide.

"KCPD. You on the stairs—show yourself." She crept down to the midfloor landing, her gun leading the way. "Hands up where I can see them."

She smelled the sweat of fear and desperation coming off the intruder as she neared the rear exit on the first floor. Maybe this was just a homeless guy who'd wandered in off the street. Nothing like discovering a hoped-for haven swarming with cops to make a guy nervous. "I'm Detective Watson with KCPD. My goal isn't to hurt you, but you're trespassing. I'd like you to identify yourself, and I need to ask you some questions."

For a few seconds, the heavy breathing stopped. Olivia focused in on the body odor wafting from the recess between the rear exit and the side of the stairs and turned. There was a guttural roar and a flash of gray before the intruder's arms swung over the railing with a metal folding chair and knocked her down the last couple of steps.

Olivia pitched forward, landing on her hip and shoulder, hitting the floor hard. Her knuckles banged against the concrete. She lost her grip on the gun and the weapon slid beyond her reach.

Instead of capitalizing on his advantage and hitting her again, the perp in the gray hoodie ran past her. But Olivia wasn't about to ignore an opportunity to take control of the situation. She kicked out her feet, twisted her legs through his and tripped him.

In a tumble of clanking metal and furious curses, her attacker went down. For the split second he was stunned by the impact with the unforgiving concrete, Olivia went after her Glock. The attacker extricated himself from the chair and pushed to his feet while she rolled toward her weapon and scooped it up.

"Hey! Stop!" A blur of denim and corduroy shot past her.

Olivia flipped over, bracing her gun between her hands. But the only shot she had was Gabriel Knight's back as he shoved her attacker against the door. "Son of a…"

She scrambled to her feet, hating that any man thought he had to save her.

"He's got a gun!" Gabe shouted.

Ah, hell. She saw it, too. "Move!"

Adrenaline or stubbornness kept him from obeying her command. With his forearm wedged against the other man's throat, Gabriel grabbed her attacker's wrist and slammed it against the wall. Once. Twice. The small Saturday night special popped free and skittered across the floor. The pesky reporter was taller and broader than the other man, blocking out any chance to get a good read on the perp beyond faded jeans and the sweatshirt. Olivia picked the snub-nosed semiautomatic up by the barrel and tucked it into the back of her belt.

She was about to put her shoulder into the reporter's ribs and knock him away from the perp when she saw the flash of steel arcing between the two men. "Knife!" She raised her gun again. "Drop it!"

Gabe Knight cursed as the smaller man shoved him into Olivia, knocking them both against the rack of folding chairs. The storage rack shifted and they wound up tangled on the floor beneath an avalanche of more chairs. The attacker flung the door open and charged into the alley behind the building before she could push Gabe off her and roll to her feet. "Get out of my way!"

"Damn it. Olivia!"

She left Gabe's outstretched fingers behind and flew out the door after the man with the knife. "Police. Stop!"

Why was it that skinny guys could always fly?

She shifted into high gear, her boots crunching gravel and debris against the asphalt. But it was no good. Even running at full tilt, he easily widened the gap between them. And she couldn't fire off even a warning shot without a clear line of sight to the cars driving past on the street beyond and whoever might be walking along the sidewalk and accidentally step into her line of fire. In a matter of seconds, like a shadow swallowed up by the bright afternoon sunlight, the perp shot around the corner and was gone.

Olivia lowered her gun, skidding to a halt as she reached the sidewalk. She glanced up and down and across the street through the beginnings of rush-hour traffic. "You lousy, lucky chameleon."

He'd either ducked inside a nearby shop or had a ride waiting for him. At the very least, he'd dropped the hood and merged with the crowd of pedestrians crossing the street as the light turned green. Since she hadn't seen his face, she had no way to identify him—not even by hair color.

"Damn you, Gabriel Knight." Breathing deeply from the wind sprint, her voice was barely a whisper. But the gun and the badge made shocked and curious passersby walk a wide berth around her. She put up her hand to reassure them she meant them no harm and holstered her gun.

But the would-be rescuer who'd gotten in the way of her doing her job was another story. Olivia raked her bangs off her forehead, blew out a heated breath and decided to tell Gabe Knight exactly where he could stick his machismo. Maybe she'd even take him in for interfering with a police officer and allowing the person she wanted to question escape.

With a decisive nod, she spun around…and plowed into the middle of Gabriel Knight's chest. There was a brief bombardment of sensations—soft corduroy and unyielding muscle; long, sinewed fingers; the faint scents of coffee and soap; heated skin beneath starched cotton—before she jerked back into her own space and shored up her defenses with the frustration and annoyance still sparking through her. Olivia planted her hands at her hips and tipped her face to his. "You followed me?"

"Are you hurt?" Gabe asked, dropping his hands from her shoulders, ignoring the accusation.

"Am I—" His nostrils flared with what must have been a fast run for him, too. The lines beside his eyes etched with concern as that piercing blue gaze swept over her. But her irritation with the man dissipated when she saw the blood dripping from his sleeve onto the asphalt at his feet. Shaking her head at the injury that could have been avoided if he'd just done what she'd said, she moved to his side to inspect the clean slice through the sleeves of his coat and shirt. "He cut you."

"I'm fine."

She'd tended enough scrapes with her three older brothers growing up that she knew that was a lie. "Let me see." She put his hand up so gravity would help control the blood flow, and peeled back the shirt cuff that was no longer white. Although the perp hadn't nicked the main vein or artery, the three-inch gash across Gabe's forearm was deep enough to need stitches. "I don't suppose your chivalry extends to carrying a handkerchief, does it?"

He smirked, reaching behind him to pull a palmful of folded white cotton from the rear pocket of his jeans. Gabe shook it open and pressed it against the wound with a wince. "You're welcome."

"For what?" Olivia took over rolling up the handkerchief and wrapping it around his forearm. "I'm going to have bruises on my tailbone and elbows, thanks to you."

"Me?" he scoffed. "That guy attacked you. He had a gun. You didn't have any backup."

"I didn't need any backup." She'd been half joking when she'd asked for the hanky. The old-fashioned habit of carrying one reminded Olivia of her Grandpa Seamus, touching a mushy place inside her…for about two seconds. Gabriel Knight was certainly no sweet, old grandfather. With a determined shrug of her shoulders, Olivia denied any softening in the animosity she felt toward this man and pulled the knot tight, drawing the skin on either side of the cut together and stemming the ooze of blood. "He was running, not fighting. I had him."

"You were on the floor."

Unlike her vocal brothers, a tightening of his lips was the only complaint Gabe made about her nursing technique. As soon as he started to lower his arm, Olivia pushed it back up. "I had the vantage point to retrieve my weapon. But you got in the way and I couldn't use my gun. Now a potential killer, or a possible witness, at the very least, is on the loose and we've got no way to track him."

"That was no innocent bystander." Gabe curled his fingers into a claw in front of her face. "My hand was on the knife with his. I've got his DNA under my nails."

Olivia released him and backed away a step. "Is that why you jumped into a situation I had under control? Just so you could swipe some DNA from a suspect?"

"Call a CSI and find out if he's in the system. At the very least, I can give a description. White male. Late twenties, early thirties. About five-nine, wiry build, receding hairline." The intensity around those cobalt eyes relaxed and he grinned at her dubious glare. "I'm a professional observer. I've got an excellent eye for detail."

The leather of her jacket creaked as she crossed her arms in front of her. He thought he'd one-upped her? Solving crimes was her job, not his. And she was damn good at it. "Yeah, well did your eye for detail notice the perp didn't have any blood on him until you got cut?

Bashing in somebody's head creates a lot of spatter. If he killed Ron Kober upstairs, then he changed his clothes and stashed them somewhere. That's probably why he was opening and closing doors." Olivia's gaze dropped to the buttons on Gabriel Knight's shirt as her thoughts took a left turn into facts that made less sense. "Why club the victim over the head when he already had two weapons on him?"

Although it had been a rhetorical question, Mr. Thought-he-knew-better-than-she-did answered, "Weapon of opportunity? Were there signs of a struggle up there?"

More like signs of a good clean-up job. Not exactly the kind of painstaking task she'd associate with their panicked, high-speed attacker. Olivia pulled her phone from her pocket. "I'm calling Detective Kincaid to give him a description of the intruder, and let him know to search the building and vehicles in the area for soiled clothes."

Fully in detective mode now, Olivia glanced around the alley, poking inside trash bags and around a stack of discarded office furniture while she reported the incident to Sawyer Kincaid. Once she hung up, she went to the nearby Dumpster to look inside. But Gabriel Knight had eavesdropped on every word; his eyes had watched every move. Now he came up beside her, lifting the lid from her hand and holding it open while she searched.

"This is a police investigation, Mr. Knight. Your services are not needed, nor are they welcome." She pointed to the stain on his coat. "You'd better go have a doctor look at that."

"If solving Kober's murder leads me to solving Danielle's, I'm not going anywhere."

A drop of blood fell from the crimson moisture

soaking his sleeve into the stinky remnants of office lunches and cleaning supplies. Groaning in resignation, she palmed his shoulder and pushed him back, catching the lid and closing it.

"You're contaminating another potential crime scene." She moved between him and the Dumpster, forcing him to retreat one more step. "Along with any DNA you *might* have picked up from your attacker."

"Your attacker, too."

Shaking her head, Olivia pulled her radio off her belt and made another call to Sawyer Kincaid and the other officers in and around the building. "This is Detective Watson. I was searching the trash in the alley behind the building. But I've got an injured civilian in need of medical attention I have to see to. I'll leave the gun the perp dropped with one of the CSI's out front, but you'll have to get somebody else to comb the area back here." She shivered beneath the unblinking intensity of Mr. Knight's piercing blue eyes. Didn't the man have business of his own to tend to besides insinuating himself into hers? "By the way, your eye for detail missed the jimmy marks on the door. That's why he had the knife, and most likely how he got inside. Still can't explain the gun, though. What I saw upstairs was a crime of passion, of opportunity. Why get your hands dirty when you can kill someone from a distance?" That probing gaze never wavered from her face, even when she drifted into her thoughts and back again. "What, you've got nothing to say for once?"

"You're not getting rid of me, Olivia." He leaned in, refusing to back down. "Either I'm part of this investigation, or I'm a long, tall shadow dogging your every move."

Feeling the chill of his real shadow falling over her

upturned face, a proximity alert went off inside her. An unexpected urge tingled through the tips of her fingers. Shaking her head, Olivia stepped to the side before she forgot she was a cop and did something stupid like slap that arrogant taunt off his face…or touch his chest to see if his heart was thumping as wildly against his rib cage as hers suddenly was.

Every self-preserving instinct she had warned her to leave Gabriel Knight and those annoying shivers he triggered right here in the alley. But Olivia had a badge and responsibilities and a hardwired sense of right and wrong she had to answer to that made her feel obligated to drive him to the ER to get his wound stitched up. "Come on. My car's out front. Keep it elevated." She took his elbow and pushed his injured forearm up and helped him hold it above the tempting location of his heart. "I'll take you to the hospital."

Chapter Three

Olivia sat on a metal stool outside the curtain of one of the ER bays at the Truman Medical Center and texted a preliminary report about the events that had transpired in the stairwell and back alley of Ron Kober's office building to her work email while the facts were still clear in her head. Although her shift was officially over, the long hours had become a habit. She'd be in before roll call meeting in the morning, too, to type her notes into a formal report for the case file.

Annoying reporter trespassed on crime scene and interfered with officer in pursuit of suspect. Recommend citing him for being a PITA.

She listened in on the more professional exchange of medical information from the other side of the curtain.

"That should do it, Mr. Knight," the lady doctor who'd introduced herself as Emilia Rodriguez-Grant intoned in a soft but succinct voice. Olivia breathed in, waiting for the words of dismissal that would signify an end to this obligation to the man who'd gotten hurt while in her custody. She heard the clank of a medical instrument being set onto a metal tray as Dr. Rodriguez-Grant continued. "Try not to get it wet for twenty-four hours. It'll leave a scar, but the stitches will keep the mark thin and less noticeable—and certainly reduce your chances of the wound becoming infected."

"Thanks, Doctor," Gabe's deep voice replied.

Scar? Wound? Olivia's lungs emptied out with a sigh of guilty resignation. She was well-trained and fully capable of defending herself against a violent suspect. But she'd only seen the folding chair and the gun. Chances were, that knife would have sliced through *her* skin if Gabriel Knight hadn't intervened.

She deleted the last two sentences from the text and replaced them with a more accurate, less petulant account.

Reporter Gabe Knight injured in assistance of officer on scene. Recommend follow-up on allegations of ties twixt Ron Kober's death and murder of Dani Reese.

After sending the text to her computer, Olivia stood, smoothing out the wrinkles in her jeans and stretching to ease the kinks in her neck and back. Her new partner, Jim Parker, was right. She'd let her emotions interfere with the calm, logical pursuit of the facts and her duty to a citizen she'd sworn to protect and serve.

Common sense meant she couldn't just dump Gabe Knight off at the hospital. As much as he'd butted heads and gotten in her way, she still needed an official witness statement from him, in case the man who'd escaped did have some bearing on Kober's murder—or the death of Gabe's fiancée. The DNA the tech from the crime lab had scraped from beneath his nails might provide a vital clue to identify the killer of one or both victims, so it had been necessary to keep him with her to maintain the chain of custody of that potential evidence. Besides, with his penchant for taking the police department to task for its shortcomings, Gabriel Knight was the last man she could risk abandoning. If he was injured worse than anything a few stitches could fix, or he blamed her for getting cut in the first place, then abandoning him at the hospital might put the department in danger of some kind of lawsuit. He'd probably make her front-page news on a dereliction of duty accusation.

Before a renewed wave of guilt and irritation could sideline her thoughts again, Olivia pulled aside the privacy curtain. "How much longer do you think you'll be…?"

Olivia's brain blanked for a split second when she saw Gabe Knight stripped to the trim waist of his blue jeans. She winced at the bruising he'd earned from his struggle with the perp, and suspected she had many similar marks herself.

But it wasn't pain—or even empathy—that quickened her pulse. *Focus on the woman in the green hospital scrubs and lab coat. Ignore the tapering T-shaped back of the man sitting on the stool beside the examination table.* So much smooth, tanned skin. She'd bet it was warm skin, too, since there was nary a goose bump, in spite of the chill from the hospital's air conditioning. *Olivia Mary Watson!*

Obeying her own mental reprimand, Olivia tore her gaze from the long stretch of Gabe Knight's bare back, forcing her attention to the petite brunette doctor. "Um, are you about done, Dr. Grant?"

The wide shoulders shrugged and Gabe rose and turned to face her. "Kept you waiting too long, Detective?"

"Hold on, Mr. Knight." Olivia's wayward eyes got some naked chest time, too, before Dr. Rodriguez-Grant tugged Gabe's arm back across the table to wrap a long piece of self-sticking gauze around his forearm. She cut the piece off the roll and patted the protective bandage into place before releasing him. "Now you're done. We just need to finish the paperwork."

Stop ogling! What was she, in junior high? Olivia raked her fingers through her hair, using the movement to distract her. She hardly qualified as a gawking innocent. It wasn't as if she'd never seen a man's naked chest before. She'd grown up with three brothers, a dad and a grandpa in the house, after all. And she'd been with Marcus for almost seven months before that relationship had blown up in her face. But Gabe Knight was taller, leaner than Marcus. His black hair was a smoky dust across some nicely honed pecs that indicated he got more exercise than sitting behind a desk all day, writing crime reports and editorials critical of KCPD.

And though she prided herself on her eye for detail, those were *not* the details she was supposed to be paying attention to. She needed to get away from this man and get a good night's sleep to recharge her energy and ability to concentrate.

"No rush. I just need to call my partner and let him know my status if I'm going to be much longer." That part was true. Jim had already texted her twice, asking if she was still with the reporter and if everything was okay. He'd gone house hunting after work with his wife, but would be there pronto if she needed him. He'd also pulled up Danielle Reese's case file and wanted to get her up to speed on the dead-end investigation. "I can go outside to make my call."

But the ER doctor stopped her before she reached the hallway. "Hang on a sec. I have some information for you, too, Detective Watson." Olivia stepped back into the treatment bay and made a point of watching Dr. Rodriguez-Grant roll the tray table out of her way and cross to a stainless steel counter to retrieve a prescription pad. "Are you up to date on your tetanus shot, Mr. Knight?"

Gabe nodded. "My work takes me out of the country sometimes, so I'm current."

"Good." The petite doctor jotted a note on the prescription pad and tore off the top sheet. "Take the full round of antibiotics and see your doctor in about ten days to remove the stitches. Of course, if it shows any signs of swelling or infection in the meantime, come back and see me."

He took the prescription note the doctor handed him and stuffed it into the front pocket of his jeans. "Thanks."

The doctor tucked her short, dark brown hair behind each ear and peeled off her sterile gloves before addressing Olivia. "If you need an official statement from me, Detective Watson, that was definitely a defensive knife wound. Something with a short, thin blade—or else we'd be in surgery reattaching tendons and ligaments instead of mending skin and muscle. I can send the official medical report for your files if you need them."

"I'd appreciate that, ma'am." Olivia quickly noted the information on her phone before reaching into the pocket behind her badge. "Here's my card."

The doctor smiled as she tucked the business card into her lab coat. "I know the address. My husband and brother both work for KCPD."

A snort of derision turned her head to the man sorting through the bundle of clothing at the examination table. Was that aggravated huff a response to learning he was surrounded by KCPD fans? Or merely a frustrated testament to the stained jacket and one-sleeved shirt that had been cut apart to gain access to the wound?

Olivia turned back to Emilia, answering with a genuine smile to distract the other woman from Gabe's possible rudeness. "I know your brother A.J. He's a very well-respected leader at the Fourth Precinct."

"Thank you. My husband, Justin Grant, is on the bomb squad—"

A knock on the outer door stopped the conversation and a blond nurse peeked through the gap in the curtains. "Dr. Grant? We have a girl in Bay 2 who's having an allergic reaction to something she ate. She's breathing on her own, but the hives—"

"I'm on my way." She was already following the nurse to another ER bay when she glanced back to Gabe and Olivia. "Excuse me."

"Of course." Suddenly, Olivia was aware of how small this curtained-off area was—and that she was alone with the department's archenemy, Gabe Knight, a man who got under her skin and into her head far too easily for her peace of mind.

Several seconds of awkward silence passed before Gabe pulled on what was left of his white shirt. "Do I need to call a cab, or will you give me a ride back to the paper?"

"Can't wait to write an exposé about me letting the perp get away? Or allowing you to get hurt?"

The dark brow over his right eye arched, his cool demeanor easily deflecting the accusations. "I was thinking more along the lines of retrieving my car from the parking garage and driving home. I jogged over to Kober's building from the *Journal* as soon as the police bulletin came through. It was just a couple of blocks from my office."

"Do you check up on every cop in the neighborhood? Or did I just get lucky that you're my responsibility today?"

He inhaled deeply, drawing her attention to the expanding hills and hollows peeking through the open front of his shirt. Really? She couldn't maintain a polite distance, or a sneering disinterest in whatever testosterone he was exuding for even two seconds? This man was the enemy of KCPD. That made him her enemy, too. Right?

He pointed to the bandage wrapped around his left forearm. "*This* is on me. I thought that fool was going to hurt you. After seeing Dani the way I did, knowing I should have done something more, I..." The sharp angles of his cheeks and jaw softened with a wry grin. "Guess I had a caveman moment."

"Caveman?" As tempted to laugh at the apt description of his earlier interference as she'd been tempted to reach out to him when his eyes had darkened at the memory of his murdered fiancée, Olivia eased up on the self-recriminations and settled for smiling in return. That was probably as good an apology as she was going to get from him—and more of a concession than she'd expected. "Me no need Og's help," she teased. "Me carry big gun."

"You carry big attitude." No denying that. And then he extended his hand across the examination table. "Thank you."

"For what?" Although her instinct was to reach out to accept a proffered hand, her caution around this man left her fingers hovering in the air.

But there was no hesitation when Gabe closed the gap between them and wrapped his hand firmly around hers. Olivia's pulse leaped as if an electrical connection had just been completed. Instead of pulling away, her fingertips squeezed around the breadth of his palm. His skin was as warm as she'd imagined, and the heat of his grip seeped beneath her skin and lit a slow, easy fire that licked its way up her arm. "For listening to my side of the story. For not leaving me there in that alley to bleed. I know holding KCPD accountable hasn't made them my biggest fan."

"Any cop would have brought you to the hospital. We don't stop to evaluate whether or not we like you if you're threatened or hurt. If someone needs our help, we do our best to deliver."

"I'll remember that next time we meet." Gabe's gaze dropped to where they still held on to each other.

Next time? Olivia quickly pulled her hand away. Was that anxiety or anticipation crawling along her spine? She supposed another encounter with the bullying reporter was inevitable, since he'd made it clear he intended to dog the Cold Case Squad's investigation into his fiancée's murder. Didn't mean she had to cling to him as though…as though she liked touching him. Still, if he could make the effort to be a little more civil and respectful, then she would do the same.

Appreciating the unspoken truce, Olivia pulled her keys from her jacket pocket and headed for the door. "I'll drive. Finish buttoning things up and meet me out in the waiting room."

Olivia strode down the hallway, flexing her fingers down at her side to alleviate the tingling awareness that lingered, determined to leave Gabe Knight and his blue eyes, warm skin and bothersome words behind her. Whatever was out of whack with her libido this evening would surely go away once she got a good night's sleep. But she'd only inhaled a couple of cool, reviving breaths when she heard the commotion out at the information desk in the lobby. "Oh, no."

She recognized all five of those urgent, worried male voices. She turned the corner and her family shifted as one, like a flock of tall, robust birds, and hurried toward her.

"Livvy?" Her father's familiar limp led the charge, his arms outstretched toward her.

There must be a sign over her head today. *Trouble magnet.* Just because she *could* handle whatever the world threw her way didn't mean she wanted to. Thomas Watson's beefy arms wrapped her up in a bear hug that lifted her onto her toes. "What happened? How badly are you hurt? I heard you took a gun off a perp."

Olivia treasured a few snug moments against her dad's chest before dropping back onto her heels and stepping away. But that only allowed space for her brothers and grandfather to circle around her. One palmed the back of her head. Another squeezed her shoulder. "It's not what you think, Dad."

Her second-oldest brother, the one with the glasses and the medical degree, brushed her bangs off her forehead and hunched down to study her eyes. "Tell me exactly what your physician said."

"You're a doctor for dead people," she groaned, referring to his position as a medical examiner with the crime lab. She swatted his hand away. "I'm not the patient, Niall. I'm fine."

Her oldest brother, Duff, wasn't buying it. "The radio report said that *you* were headed to the ER."

"Damn it, guys. If you're going to eavesdrop on the police scanner, make sure you've got your information right. I brought in a…" What exactly was Gabriel Knight? A suspect? A lead on a murder investigation?

A not-so-innocent bystander? "I brought in a person of interest who is…helping with a case. He got injured at a crime scene late this afternoon."

Her father propped his hands at his waist and shook his head, needing a little more convincing for the fear to dissipate. "But you're okay? You missed dinner. Dad made his Guinness bread and stew. You never miss that."

"Oh." She smiled at the silver-haired gentleman beside her father. "Sorry, Grandpa. I lost track of the time. Did you save me a slice?"

Seamus Watson released his double grip on his cane and squeezed her hand. "Of course, sweetie."

Keir, the brother closest in age to her, loosened the knot of his tie. "I heard you were in pursuit of an armed suspect. Are you sure you're okay?"

"A couple of bruises and a wounded ego for letting the guy I was chasing get away. But I'm fine." She beamed a reassuring smile to each member of her close-knit family before reaching up to smooth the rumpled collar of her father's blue chambray shirt. "Now you want to get the gang out of here? I'm sure somebody in this family besides me has to work in the morning. I don't know about any of you, but I'm exhausted. Let's all go to our respective homes, and I promise I'll swing by the house tomorrow morning." She winked to the eighty-year-old sweetheart beside her dad. Seamus had always been her go-to guy when she needed someone in the family to listen to her. "A toasty piece of Grandpa's bread and an over-easy egg to dip it in is my favorite breakfast."

"I'm glad it was just a misunderstanding and that you're all right." His old-country lilt was as softly reassuring as the sweet peck on the cheek he gave her. "I'll have breakfast hot and ready for you. Good night, Livvy."

"Good night, Grandpa."

They were in the midst of hugs and good-nights and going on their way when her father puffed up to his full height and glared over Olivia's shoulder. "This SOB is your person of interest?"

Olivia didn't have to turn to know that Gabe had come up behind her. She was learning to recognize him by the size of his shadow and the subtle scent that was a mix of soap and starch and now a tinge of antiseptic. And that deep-pitched voice with the cynical undertones was unmistakable.

"Is this the rest of your family, Detective?"

The *rest* of her family? Although the question didn't quite make sense, Olivia nodded. Every loud, overprotective, stubborn Irish man belonged to her. "These are my guys."

Gabe stepped up beside her, his gaze sweeping the circle of her family. "Let me guess, you're *all* cops?"

"Kansas City's Finest." Her father's shoulders came back proudly as he made the claim. "Not that you'd care."

Of course, they'd recognize the department's harshest critic—and be less than pleased to learn he was the man she'd brought to the ER. She didn't suppose introductions would alleviate the tension rising around her, but it couldn't hurt to turn the rumored enemy into an actual person with a name and a stitched-up arm—or to let Gabe know just how proud she was of her family and their accomplishments.

"Dad, this is Gabriel Knight. You probably recognize his name from the *Kansas City Journal.* My father, Thomas Watson. Dad retired a senior detective from the department a couple years ago. This is my grandfather, Seamus, a longtime desk sergeant, also KCPD, retired." There was no sense adding a title to the other introductions—they all wore the badges and ME card from their respective departments proudly on display. "My brothers, Duff, Niall and Keir."

If anything, the animosity in the air thickened. Her father looked as grim as she'd ever seen him. "Introductions aren't necessary, Livvy. We've met."

She swiveled her gaze up to Gabe. He wasn't smiling, either. He nodded, confirming her dad's icy statement. "Watson. When I met your daughter, I wasn't expecting to run into you. Maybe I just didn't want to."

"How do you two know each other?" Olivia asked.

"Your father was the cop who investigated Dani's murder."

Chapter Four

"What were you thinking?"

The fidgety young man sitting in the plush chair on the other side of the desk was crawling out of his skin as he listened to the calmer voice.

"You could have ruined everything. I told you I'd take care of it."

"I had to do something," the young man argued.

"No, you didn't. If you'd been caught, your actions would have jeopardized everything we've worked for."

"Are you angry with me?"

"Surprised. Maybe a little disappointed." That sucked the nervous energy right out of him. "I thought you trusted me."

"I do. But I can't go to prison." The young man scratched at the marks on the back of his hand. He needed a shave, some sleep, and most likely, a fix. "I don't think I could handle that. What if Mr. Kober talked?"

"He won't now, will he? And he wouldn't have. As I said, everything is as it should be, according to my plan. I'm taking care of the situation, just as I'm taking care of you." The host unlocked the top right drawer of the desk and reached inside to pull out a small envelope filled with cash. The young man's eyes rounded like saucers and he nearly licked his chapped lips in anticipation. "You know I shouldn't give you this. It's not much, just enough to tide you over for a few days."

The young man leaned forward in his chair. "I can't get any money right now. It's all tied up."

"I'm sure you feel frustrated about that."

"Helpless is more like it. When I saw on TV that Senator McCoy was running for reelection, and that Mr. Kober was being investigated, I had to do something. He knew about that woman. What if he knew about me, too?" The nerves were kicking in again. "I could lose what little I have left. If the truth comes out…"

This misguided, troubled young man had no real understanding of the truth. "You wouldn't want your family to find out what you've done, would you?"

His chair rattled against the floor as he visibly shook. "No."

"Then trust me. Just like you have all along. I've taken good care of you, haven't I? I've helped you."

His brown eyes fixated on the envelope. "Yeah."

"When you listen to me and do as I suggest, everything is fine?"

The young man nodded.

"Then listen to me now." The host slipped the envelope across the desk and the young man snatched it up and stuffed it inside his jacket. "It's more important than ever that you don't draw any attention to yourself. Go home to your family. Clean yourself up. Get back to your work and leave everything to me. I've got it all under control—"

"*I* want to be in control." Angry tears dotted his cheeks as the young man pounded his fist on top of the desk. "I'm not in control of my own life, anymore."

The host inhaled a deep breath and exhaled the irritation this visitor was causing. "That will come in time. I promise you. We can't solve all your problems in one day."

"I'm trying to do the right thing."

"I know. But until you learn to make the best choices for yourself, you need to listen to me. Do what I tell you and everything will be fine. Do you understand that?"

The young man's head jerked with a nod.

"Good."

OLIVIA TILTED HER EYES to the rearview mirror and drummed her fingers on the Explorer's steering wheel. It was still there.

The low-slung muscle car with the tinted windows sat two vehicles behind her, waiting at the same stoplight. Normally, she would have dismissed several sightings of the same car on the way to work as a comrade in arms, battling rush-hour traffic en route to his or her job in downtown Kansas City.

But she didn't like not being able to get some description of the driver—gender, age, ethnicity. She didn't like having her vision so obscured by traffic that she couldn't get a license plate number. She especially didn't like spotting the same car cruising past her father's house long before she'd pulled onto the Interstate to merge with the thousands of other cars swarming into the city this morning. And seeing the same black car pull off on the same exit to enter the heart of downtown raised every hackle at the nape of her neck.

Someone was following her.

At least, that's what every instinct that had been on hyperalert since yesterday afternoon was trying to tell her.

Yesterday, she'd made a mental note of the silver SUV

Gabe Knight drove when she dropped him off. Although her goodbye and *Don't call me, I'll call you* had been firm and to the point, she wouldn't put it past him to tail her, in hopes of finding out information on his fiancée's murder. But why switch vehicles? She knew he had an obsessive interest in the case. But other than not sharing the connection he had to her father, he'd seemed like a straightforward kind of guy. This had to be something else, right?

But she'd been wrong about Ron Kober's murder being a wasted errand for her and Jim. She'd been wrong about the man in the stairwell intending no harm. She might even have been wrong about Gabriel Knight being the coldhearted villain the rest of the department believed him to be.

Maybe yesterday hadn't been a fluke, and her people-reading radar was on the fritz. She could be wrong about Mr. Muscle Car back there, too. But just to test a theory...

As soon as the light changed, Olivia nosed her Explorer into the turn lane and made a sharp left without signaling. She raised an apologetic hand at the honks of protest and cruised on through the intersection. Good. The driver in the black car wasn't laying on the horn or making any sudden moves to turn the corner after her.

Huffing out the breath she must have been holding, Olivia relaxed her grip around the steering wheel and merged into traffic to double back to her original route. So maybe the car wasn't following her. If it showed up again between here and the KCPD parking garage, she could always stick the siren on her roof and swing around to make a traffic stop and get her questions answered. But for now, she could drop her guard.

Olivia drove the last six blocks without another sighting of the black car. Not Gabe Knight. Not a threat. Her suspicion eased enough to chalk up the notion she was being followed to coincidence. Either a car dealer had made a fortune selling more than one customized car, or the driver was simply traveling the same route that she was. Stranger things had happened.

With a little rational thought, Olivia had her emotional armor firmly back in place as she pulled into the KCPD parking garage. She locked up her SUV and headed down the stairs, joining the migration of personnel reporting in for morning duty.

The sun in the east was warm, peeking between the tall buildings of downtown Kansas City. The newly planted dogwood trees in front of the limestone building that served as both Fourth Precinct and administrative headquarters were budding out. Her tummy was full of Grandpa Seamus's good cooking. Her dad had tolerated her questions about Dani Reese's murder—even though any mention of Gabe Knight still seemed to get him hot under the collar. The irksome conflicts that had messed up yesterday for her were just that—yesterday's business. She was nothing if not resilient. Feeling stronger and smarter and more sure of herself this morning, Olivia looked forward to seeing friends and getting some solid investigative work done.

The building's public facade was feeling more familiar, too, with several months of construction and re-installation and upgrades to the security system finally complete. The entryway at the top of the gray granite steps had been rebuilt after a tornado the previous summer had toppled stately pine trees and tossed a vehicle through the front doors. There were new benches out front, new shine to the steel framing the double doors, manufacturer stickers still stuck to the glass that had recently been replaced. But despite the torn-up landscaping, shattered windows and damaged antennae and satellite dishes on the roof that had been repaired or replaced, the concrete-and-steel heart of the ninety-year-old building remained intact.

Olivia wished the officer she'd been chatting with a good day and took a detour to one of the benches. Another departmental fixture that hadn't changed much was Max Krolikowski. Olivia grinned at the burly blond detective in the black leather blazer reclining against the back of the bench, with one foot propped up on the opposite knee and a Churchill-style cigar pinched between his lips. The uniform had changed as he'd moved from assignment to assignment, but now that the two were both working in the cold case unit, she'd learned that the former army sergeant wasn't as antisocial and bad for the department's public image as he'd like most people to believe.

He muttered a curse that made her smile when he saw her approach, sat up straight and pulled the flattened tip of the cigar from his mouth. "Here it comes," he growled.

Olivia sat on the bench beside him. "I thought you gave up smoking."

Although he wasn't any older than her brother Duff, Max had his grumpy-old-man shtick down to an art form. "Do you see a match or lighter on me?"

"Well, I can't imagine eating that stogie is any better for you." She eyed the trash can beside him. "Why don't you just throw it away?"

"Mind your own business, Liv." He flicked the cigar into the trash, then pulled two more wrapped smokes from his chest pocket to show her how ornery he could be. "I'm not one of your brothers. You don't have to take care of me."

Uh-huh. That's why there was a stain from breakfast,

or maybe even last night's dinner, peeking from behind the badge hanging at the front of his shirt.

Olivia checked her watch and stood. "You know I only nag because I care about you."

"Bite me."

Olivia laughed. "Come on. Roll call is about to start. Then we have our briefing with Lieutenant Rafferty-Taylor. I've got a six-year-old murder case I want to take another look at."

He tucked the cigars inside the front of his jacket and dropped his work-booted foot to the pavement. "Sounds like reason enough to start my day."

A shadow fell over Olivia and she shivered. But that rush of anticipation at the idea of butting heads with Gabriel Knight again quickly died when she faced familiar cocoa-brown eyes that had once made her heart skip a beat. Marcus Brower's perfect white smile lit up his face with a grin. "Hey, look, it's Beauty and the Beast."

Her heart still skipped a beat. But it was a jolt of surprise, of not being prepared to fend off the inevitable suspicion and remembered humiliation pounding through her veins. Even if the pain wasn't as intense as it had once been, it took Olivia a deep breath and a needless adjusting of the zippers on her teal leather jacket to paste a wry smile on her own face and answer. "Good morning, Marcus."

He winked. "Morning, babe."

What Max Krolikowski lacked in manners, he made up for in loyalty. While Olivia bristled at the endearment, her grousing coworker stood up beside her. "We were just leaving."

But Marcus's hand on her arm stopped her. "Hey, Liv. We see each other every day, but we never talk. Can we? Are you free for lunch?"

"No."

"Dinner?"

She shook her head. "I'm busy."

"Don't blow me off. I know you're not seeing anyone."

"That doesn't mean I don't have a life." She jerked her arm from his grasp. "I've got plans." And by dinner tonight, she hoped that pathetic little lie would be the truth.

"Okay, so you're not purposely avoiding me." A dimple appeared at the corner of his mouth as the charming smile reappeared. "Morning, noon or night—you tell me when, and I'll be there. I don't like the way we left things."

An image of a naked Marcus rolling around on *their* bed with the receptionist from his dentist's office or the gym or wherever he'd picked up that latest conquest blipped through her mind. Olivia resolutely slammed the door on that memory and backed up a step to follow Max. "There's nothing more to say. You made your choice."

He caught the tips of her fingers with his, lightly hanging on. "We were good friends—partners—before I screwed up. I miss the way we used to be. I made a mistake. I want to fix that."

Max leveled his icy gaze over Olivia's shoulder. "We've got meetings to get to, sunshine. So do you."

The charm bled from Marcus's tone. "Was I talking to you, Krolikowski? Bug off."

Olivia extricated her fingers from Marcus's pseudo-grasp and pushed Max on up the stairs before a real argument with an unwanted audience could start. "Let's go."

"I'm not giving up on this, Liv," Marcus called after

her. "I was a better person when I was with you. I owe you an explanation."

A spurt of her own temper rose like bile in her throat. The explanation was simple. Marcus was a player. His ability to say no to any flirtatious come-on when they'd been together wasn't any stronger than his ability to grasp the meaning of the word right now. Yes, she'd been good for him—but the reverse wasn't true. She didn't need a private heart-to-heart to understand that.

She spun around to let Marcus know exactly when she'd be willing to listen to any excuse he had to say. Never. "You don't owe me any…"

But the snarky rebuttal died on her lips. Her new partner, Jim Parker, had come up behind Marcus. "Is there a problem here?"

"No." Great. Just what she needed—her new partner discovering what a naive idiot she'd been with her old one. Olivia quickly excused herself, pushing past Max to shove open the front door. "I'm going to work, even if no one else is."

A look from Max and Jim wisely kept Marcus from joining them on the elevator up to the third floor. Olivia pushed the button and pretended the number three lighting up was the most interesting thing in the world. Max snorted and drifted to the back of the elevator to lean against the railing. "Does anything ever come out of that guy's mouth that isn't loaded with lies?"

When she didn't respond, Jim turned to Max. "Is there an issue with Detective Brower I should know about?"

"Liv used to be his partner over in Vice until Lieutenant Rafferty-Taylor recruited her for the Cold Case Squad."

Olivia was only partially aware of being the topic

of conversation as she pulled her hand away from the panel. She curled her fingers into her palm, caught off guard by a remembered touch. But it wasn't that cutesy little coupling of fingertips outside when Marcus had stopped her—or even the brush of his lover's hand across her body months earlier. She was remembering a firmer touch—a handshake, of all things—with Gabriel Knight. An unapologetic stamp of skin on skin. Strong. Warm. Lingering.

She trembled with a curious awareness that felt as vivid now as it had last night at the hospital.

"Is there bad blood between you two?" Jim asked.

Instead of answering, Olivia flattened her palm against the cool leather of her jacket and rubbed the back of her knuckles as if her right hand had somehow betrayed her. Oh, man. She was in trouble. Despite the stress Gabe Knight had caused, he'd somehow awakened hormones she thought had been in a permanent coma after tossing Marcus out of her life. She was totally screwed with both her family and her coworkers if she even hinted that she might be attracted to the reporter.

And Max was already feeling too chatty about her last relationship disaster to risk getting razzed about Gabriel Knight. "That's right." Max snapped his fingers at Jim. "You were working with the bureau task force for a while there. You're out of the loop. Brower and Liv used to be an item. For a few months. Pretty hot and heavy before she transferred."

"Shut up, Max."

But she couldn't get the hint through Max's thick skull. "I'm glad she wised up and ended it. You know, for a while there, I thought I was going to have to rent a monkey suit and go to a wedding."

She turned and glared.

Max had the good sense to raise a placating hand in apology as the elevator slowed. "Shutting up now." But not really. He leaned his head confidentially toward Jim. "You know, people think I'm the one you have to watch out for on our squad since I've been around so long and I've seen everything. Or they worry about Dixon because he's got that big, bad tough-guy thing going on." Max pointed a finger at her. "*She's* the one who'll break you in two if you cross her. I recommend staying on her good side."

"Good to know." Jim gave a hesitant agreement, looking from one detective to the other.

Olivia turned away, rubbing at the seed of a headache throbbing in her temple. "Take your own advice, Max."

The burly detective chuckled. "You know I love ya, Liv."

The elevator bell dinged, announcing their arrival on the third floor. "Thank God."

Olivia dashed out, leaving the gossip and that uncomfortable fascination with Gabe Knight behind her. She headed straight for a cup of coffee in the break room, hoping to claim a few minutes of peace and quiet, but she couldn't shake Max and Jim, their questions or teasing until the roll call meeting was called to order.

After the half-hour meeting to discuss cases of department-wide concern, announce BOLOs and sign-ups for the upcoming annual baseball game against the fire department, Olivia, Jim, Max and Trent Dixon, the fourth detective assigned to their unit, filed into Ginny Rafferty-Taylor's office. Lieutenant Rafferty-Taylor had recently been promoted from her work as a homicide detective. But the petite blonde had slipped right into command of the cold case unit with an intelligence and air of authority that Olivia not only respected, but aspired to in her own law-enforcement career.

In contrast to the senior officer's professional, no-nonsense demeanor, Lieutenant Rafferty-Taylor's office was decorated with framed artwork painted by her kids. A trifold picture frame on the shelf behind her showed a photo of her and her husband, Brett, a big, beefy man whose hair was as dark as hers was silvery-blonde, along with individual pictures of their daughter and son, who were carbon copies of their mother and father, respectively.

Somehow the lieutenant had found that equanimity between being a decorated career officer and being a woman with a life outside of work. Olivia had yet to figure out that balance for herself. And after her foolish affair with Marcus, she had a feeling she was further than ever from finding that happily ever after. So she concentrated on the part of her life that she knew she was good at—being an investigator who could ferret out the truth when others around her could not.

After listening to updates on other cases the team was working, Olivia briefed the team on the events of yesterday afternoon surrounding Ron Kober's murder.

"Wait a minute." Max's partner, Trent Dixon, a former college football player, picked up the newspaper he'd set aside and unfolded it on top of the small conference table. He tapped the article he'd been looking for and Olivia leaned over to read it. "Gabe Knight's column says that Ron Kober was subpoenaed to testify before the State Senate Ethics Commission regarding potential campaign fraud during Senator McCoy's last run for election. Do we think his killer wanted to shut him up?"

Information Specialist Katie Rinaldi sat at the end of the table with her laptop, going back and forth between typing notes and the ongoing project of inputting updates on the unsolved case records she was transferring from paper files into the computer database. She tucked the shoulder-length strands of her chestnut hair behind her ears. "Should I be copying Detectives Kincaid and Hendricks on our discussion if they're working Mr. Kober's murder?"

"Not yet." Lieutenant Rafferty-Taylor sat at the opposite end of the table. "If we find anything substantive, we will. But until then, Kober isn't our case. Jim, I see you pulled the file on the Danielle Reese murder from six years back. Did we get a new lead there?"

"That was my request, ma'am," Olivia answered. "I've got a lead that suggests Ron Kober had a connection to the story Dani Reese was writing at the time of her murder. I can't say that he's her killer, but I'd like to follow up on it."

"Katie, is Ms. Reese's file in the system yet?" Ginny asked.

"Yes, ma'am."

"Pull it up." Ginny typed a note on her own laptop before raising her gaze. "What's your lead?"

Olivia picked up the folded newspaper and pointed to the byline. "Gabriel Knight. He claims that Dani was getting inside information about a link between Leland Asher and Senator McCoy's election for an article she was writing. Kober was McCoy's campaign manager at the time of her murder. If anyone had inside information on a crime boss's support of a candidate, it'd be Kober."

"And how does Mr. Knight know this?"

"Well, he suspects." Olivia left out the fiancée part and stuck to the more important facts. "Dani Reese was a junior reporter at the *Kansas City Journal.* He was mentoring her, and read some of her notes on the story before she died."

Max sat forward in his chair across the table, looking dubious about the reporter's cooperation. "Can we get those notes?"

"I hope so. I know Mr. Knight isn't a fan of the department, but this case is important to him. I intend to ask him."

Lieutenant Rafferty-Taylor nodded, approving the reopening of the case. "I'm all for anything we can pin on Asher to put him away. And some good press from Mr. Knight can't hurt any of us. Let's talk it out."

Katie's work on entering data on cold cases dating back to the 1800s made it easier to cross-reference information from different investigations. She'd started, of course, with the most recent cases, so everything the department had on Danielle Reese's murder was there to access. But she pulled her bottom lip between her teeth and frowned as she skimmed the screen. "There's not much here. The ME's report. Witness statements from the men who found her. According to the ballistics, the gun used to kill her was a .25 caliber semiautomatic. But no murder weapon was ever recovered."

Jim skimmed the same information in the paper file he'd picked up yesterday. "No wonder the UNSUB had to shoot her three times. A little gun like that doesn't carry a big punch. Unless he wanted her to suffer."

"Maybe she knew her killer," Trent suggested. "And he didn't want her to die fast."

Max leaned back in his chair. "Or Asher told his man to stage the scene so it wouldn't look like a hit. Maybe Senator McCoy hired someone to silence her."

The lieutenant reminded them of the original investigation. "In that part of town, it very well could have been a robbery. If she struggled with her assailant, he might have panicked. But these are all just theories. I won't go to the DA unless we have a viable suspect and real proof."

Katie raised her eyebrows. "Yeah, Uncle Dwight is a stickler for that kind of thing," she added as her fingers flew over the keyboard, referring to the man who had saved her life when she was a teenager and become her legal guardian after marrying Katie's aunt.

Olivia agreed that any of the three scenarios was plausible, yet unprovable at this point. "Do we still have anything in evidence?"

Katie read the short list off the screen. "Crime scene photos. Bullets the ME removed. The victim's clothes, purse and a few items from her glove compartment. The officers on the scene said the insurance cards, registration and other paperwork were missing—maybe to delay identifying the victim, maybe as part of the carjacking—or else they just blew away. The notes here say there was a thunderstorm the night of her death. She wasn't found until the next day, and the doors, trunk and glove box were all open."

Max muttered a curse. "The wind and rain probably compromised the majority of any circumstantial evidence that was there."

"Do we still have Ms. Reese's car?" Lieutenant Rafferty-Taylor asked.

Katie nodded. "It's in Impound."

"Wait a sec. Go back. We have her purse in evidence?" Olivia looked at the young single mom turned computer wiz. "Why would KCPD investigate her death as a robbery if her purse was still there? What else was missing?"

"Her wallet and phone weren't in her bag or pockets.

The investigator's report says she wasn't wearing any jewelry, but she had pierced ears. Marks from a ring and watch that were gone, too. They assumed the jewelry was stolen. No notation that any of it was ever recovered." Katie looked up from the screen, her blue eyes wide with curiosity. "Hey, Liv. Is this your dad's signature on the file?"

Olivia exhaled a reluctant sigh and nodded. She hoped the personal connection wouldn't put her in dutch with the lieutenant. "I didn't know this was his case until last night. We chatted some this morning. He said it was the only one he and his partner Al Junkert never solved. There just wasn't enough evidence to go on. And no one with discernible motive."

If Ginny Rafferty-Taylor was concerned about Olivia's objectivity, she didn't show it. "Was Gabriel Knight involved with the case back then? Did he tell your father his suspicions about Leland Asher and Senator McCoy?"

"Dad mentioned it." Her father had also said that exploring Gabe's suggestion had led to a dead end, including a blanket denial of even knowing Dani Reese from the senator's office, and an unpleasant run-in with one of Asher's men. But that had ended with nothing more than a disorderly conduct charge. "Dad said they couldn't match ballistics to any of the guns owned by Leland Asher and his crew. And they all had alibis Dad couldn't break. Either proof of being out of town, or a family wedding with video that put the rest of them, including Leland Asher, at the reception during the time of the murder."

"Any records of Asher making big withdrawals around the time of the murder?" Jim asked.

Olivia shook her head, knowing what he was getting at. "If he hired a hit man, there was no paper trail that Dad or Al could find."

Gabe Knight's claims were looking less credible by the minute. Maybe, as her father said, the collusion story and cover-up was nothing more than a grieving fiancé grasping at straws. Danielle Reese could very well have been the victim of a random carjacking. Although Gabe had seemed so certain that his fiancée's death was some kind of mob connection cover-up that Olivia had believed him enough to bring Dani's case to the team.

And, maybe there was a little bit of Irish vindication running through her veins. If she could solve this case for her dad, it might make his forced retirement after a career-ending injury a little easier to enjoy.

"Are we a go on reopening Dani Reese's murder?" Olivia asked, watching her supervisor's gray-blue eyes for approval.

The lieutenant closed her laptop, signaling that the meeting was winding down. "Sounds like our type of investigation. Olivia, you take the lead. Reinterview any suspects and the men who found her, look at the crime scene, nail down the motive—you know the drill."

"Yes, ma'am." Olivia rose and pulled her jacket off the back of her chair. "I can follow up with Dad—see if he's got any insights that might not be in the records."

Jim jotted a line on his notepad and closed it. "I'll go over to storage and pull the evidence box. We can look at everything with fresh eyes. If there are any trace samples, I'll find out if there are new tests the lab can run on them."

Ginny Rafferty-Taylor shrugged into her sky-blue blazer. "If this was a robbery, let's prove it. If not, our best lead is to talk to the man who knew our victim best.

See if we can put our hands on those notes she allegedly kept and find a motive there."

"Best lead, as in Gabriel Knight?"

The lieutenant nodded. "You've already established a rapport. Talk to him. Let's make him KCPD's friend again. We need to get a look at the story Dani Reese was writing."

Olivia adjusted her jacket over the white blouse she wore before answering. Her fingers hadn't just started tingling at the mention of Gabe's name, had they?

Thankfully, no one seemed to notice her hesitation. There was a chorus of *yes, ma'am*s as they shut down computers and pushed away from the table.

"I expect regular updates," Ginny reminded them. "Keep in touch."

"Trent?" Katie set her laptop on the table and hurried past Olivia to reach the dark-haired muscle man before he left the room. "Tyler has Little League tryouts this weekend. I was wondering if you could help him with his swing? This is his first year playing regular ball instead of hitting off the tee. I'll throw in a home-cooked meal for your trouble."

"Baseball's not my sport," the big man conceded. But he smiled at the mention of Katie's son. "You know how much I like hanging out with the little guy, though. I'll give it a shot. Saturday okay?"

While the computer genius and the detective worked out the details of their weekend afternoon, Jim circled around the table to speak to Olivia. "I've picked up that Knight isn't your favorite person. Want me to go with you?"

Adjusting the cuffs and collar of her blouse, Olivia frowned. "I thought you and Natalie had an appointment with a Realtor about making an offer on that house you two saw yesterday."

"I'll postpone the meeting."

"Don't be ridiculous. I can handle Gabe Knight on my own." She tugged on the badge hanging around her neck. "The day I can't conduct an interview is the day I need to turn this in."

"You sure you're not just trying to go solo without me again? You can't break me in if we don't spend time working together." Although there was a teasing smile in his green eyes, she had a feeling he was half serious.

"That's not it." Still, Jim was right—they hadn't quite found their investigative rhythm yet. And she didn't want to be distracted with working a new partner into the equation when she met with Gabe Knight. "Like Ginny said, I've developed a rapport with him. He may not like any of us, but I think he'll talk to me." If Gabe's willingness to work with her meant the difference in solving the crime, then she'd deal with his stubbornness, her family's reservations against the man—even those illogical frissons of awareness he'd awakened in her—and make him her best friend. "If Knight gives me any grief, Max said I'm scary enough to take him down if I have to."

The grumpy detective chuckled as he followed them out the door. "You got that right."

Olivia smiled. Max was too much of a teddy bear beneath the grizzly exterior to stay mad at him for long. Jim was starting to grow on her, too. "Besides, if I need you, I've got your number."

Jim paused before heading over to the bank of elevators. "Use it. I'm here to back you up."

Maybe if he kept saying that, she might actually learn to believe in a partner again. "Thanks, Jim. Let me know what you find in the evidence box. Good luck with the house."

Max folded his arms across his barrel chest, blocking her path as he scratched at the pale stubble on his chin. "You want me to go with you? I'm not afraid of Knight."

Even though she could tell that his offer of support was sincere, Olivia let him off the hook with a teasing punch to the arm. "You're not one of my brothers, remember? I don't need you lookin' out for me. Go eat a cigar."

"Sounds yummy." Trent came out of the lieutenant's office with a sarcastic drawl and clapped Max on the shoulder. "You and me are taking a trip to Impound."

"Yippee," Max answered in a monotone. "We get the stinky old car." But he walked backward, following his partner's exit without further complaint. "Brower was a butthead for cheating on you, Liv."

"I know."

"I only told Jim because he needs to have your back in case Brower is dumb enough to think he can talk you into forgiving him or something."

"I know that, too. Get to work."

With Katie Rinaldi and Ginny Rafferty-Taylor going over data in the lieutenant's office, and the guys on the team out pursuing their assignments, Olivia finally got her peace and quiet. For a few moments. Then the cacophony of the Fourth Precinct's third-floor Detectives Division registered. Dozens of conversations, phones ringing, keyboards clicking and printers and other machines whirring as they spit out information filled her ears and wore at her nerves.

But, since running home for a hot bubble bath or a primal scream in the middle of the room probably weren't the best strategies for coping with this morning's stress, Olivia inhaled a deep breath and marched past the cubicle where her desk faced Jim's and pushed open the door to the now empty conference room. She exhaled the calming breath and rallied her patience. The last thing she needed was to lose her focus when she talked to Gabriel Knight.

Turning to keep watch through the glass windows on either side of the door, Olivia pulled up the number she'd programmed in yesterday and called Gabe.

A terse, low-pitched voice answered. "Knight."

Sucker. Her nostrils flared with a quick breath. Why couldn't she shake this skittish, way-too-feminine-for-her-liking thing about the man? She must have some kind of masochistic streak to be attracted to men who were trouble for her.

Olivia ignored the deep voice that skittered against her eardrums and focused on the muffled noises of a busy metropolitan newspaper office in the background. "Good morning, Mr. Knight. This is Detective Watson, KCPD. I need to speak to you. In person. Are you at work? I could meet you at your office or you could come to the station."

He answered with a long pause that made her wonder if he'd been interrupted at his end of the call. Then the noise in the background went silent and she suspected he'd closed the door to his office, turning this into a private conversation. "Are you reopening Dani's murder?"

Before she could answer, broad shoulders and dark hair appeared in the window. Marcus flashed his dimpled smile and rapped on the glass. "You free?"

Olivia frowned, hating the interruption, and frankly, hating him at that moment. She pointed to the phone. "No."

"Excuse me?" a deep voice challenged in her ear.

Oh, damn.

"Sorry, I…" She turned the lock on the doorknob and turned her back on Marcus. "That was for someone here. Yes, we're reopening the case. I need to ask you some questions—go over everything you know about your fiancée's murder."

"Two things, Olivia." She could feel Marcus's dark eyes drilling her through the glass, and suspected his cajoling smile had disappeared. But, for some reason, her ex's frustration with her didn't bother her as much as the displeasure tingeing the man's voice on the phone. "One, it's Gabe. And two? You'd better be bringing your *A* game to this investigation. I'll see you when you get here."

Chapter Five

Gabe spotted the rich blue-green jacket from the corner of his eye. He looked up from the article he was typing on his computer and watched Olivia Watson through the windows of his office. She said something to the receptionist who pointed in his direction, toward the line of private rooms surrounding the *Journal*'s news and editorial department's main floor, and raised her mysterious eyes to meet his.

When their gazes met, she gave him a slight nod before clipping the badge she'd shown the receptionist back onto the chain she wore. Olivia shot her fingers through that sexy crop of short, dark hair, steeled her shoulders and strode through the jungle of desks, reporters, columnists, runners and techs with a certainty of purpose that was at once professionally confident and surprisingly hot. At least, that jump in his pulse seemed to think so.

"I'm finally getting you justice, Dani," he whispered to the ghosts of the past that filled the air around him. "One way or another." After saving his story and clearing the computer screen, Gabe stood, smoothing the shirt sleeves he'd rolled up to his elbows. When the leggy detective paused in the open doorway, he extended his hand and circled around the desk to greet her. "Olivia."

"Gabe." She folded her firm grip into his. He liked

that she used his name the way he'd asked without making a big deal out of it. "This is a noisy place."

"Hence, the private office."

"You made it sound as though stopping by anytime was okay. So here I am."

"Now is fine. We already put tomorrow morning's paper to bed and I'm working ahead." Here they stood, sharing another handshake. Another linger. His thumb grazed over the soft bump of her knuckles. Olivia's skin was smooth, warm. Her eyes this afternoon were a muted shade of gray dotted with green-and-gold specks that darkened the longer he held on to her.

So let go already. This is a business meeting, not a blind date.

"How's the arm?" Olivia asked, showing more sense than he had by pulling away and stepping into his office.

He kept his back to her, needing a few seconds to compartmentalize this potent interest in the lady detective and concentrate on the reason he'd agreed to see her in the first place—getting to the truth about Dani's killer. Only then did he turn, waving his fingers in the air to prove their dexterity, despite the bandage wrapped around his forearm. "A little sore. But as long as I can type, I'm good." He pointed to her left wrist, indicating the violet bruise peeking out beneath the cuff of her white blouse. "Looks like you got a little banged up, too."

"I'll live."

"Coffee?" he offered.

"Sure. With cream if you have it." He pointed to one of the guest chairs and invited her to sit while he headed out to the break room.

By the time he returned with two insulated cups, Gabe had let enough of his cynicism and doubt creep back into his thoughts to temper his libido. He closed the door with his foot to block out the noise from the main room and handed Olivia her drink. "So where do we start?"

Gabe resumed his seat behind his desk while Olivia popped open her lid to swirl the coffee and creamer together and allow some of the steam to escape. "At the beginning. When we don't have a clear lead, we usually look at the victim. What can you tell me about Danielle Reese?"

"Looked like an angel. She liked baking and knitting and having fresh flowers around the condo. But that was more about being an overachiever than a homebody. She never could sit still. She came from a small town in Kansas—Cottonwood Falls. Got her journalism degree at the University of Missouri and moved to the big city, determined to be a success and never have to go back to where she came from. She loved her parents, but the pace of a small town bored her. She wanted the diversity and excitement of the city and the job. She wanted a Pulitzer. She wanted to make a difference."

Olivia pressed the lid back onto her coffee and took a sip. "Did she normally investigate suspected connections between organized crime and politics?"

Gabe shook his head, remembering the first time he'd seen the dewy-faced blonde lugging an armload of boxes to her desk in the middle of the reporters' pool. "She was willing to learn her craft, build her reputation. She took every assignment from covering wedding announcements to interviewing local human interest stories. But she always wanted to get into hard news."

"That's when you started mentoring her?"

"Yeah. I let her tag along on some of the tamer assignments I had—reporting on school bond debates, weather stories like the floods we had a few years back.

She'd draft a story and I'd read it, tweak it. I shared a couple of bylines with her." Dani's eagerness to learn and excel, her youthful energy and attentiveness had been an aphrodisiac to his ego. "Pretty soon she didn't need me to get the story or write it. By then, things had gotten personal between us. I proposed. She accepted."

Olivia set her cup on the edge of the desk and pulled her phone from her pocket, ostensibly to type in details of their conversation. "So you moved in together and continued your Svengali relationship with her. On the sly. You said you had to sneak a look at her notes? That she was keeping that last investigation a secret? Even from you?" She paused in her typing to meet his gaze.

He resented the Svengali allusion. Sure, maybe their relationship had started out like that, but once they became a couple, he and Dani had been equal partners. There'd been nothing more he could teach her. It wasn't until the late nights and the missed dinners and the calls that went straight to voice mail that he'd gotten worried enough to find out what she was keeping from him. And then he realized he hadn't taught her nearly enough about surviving a dangerous investigation.

Gabe took a drink that scalded the guilt from his throat. "Do you even know what she looked like?"

Olivia shook her head. "Just the crime scene photos. And those…are pretty rough."

That was an understatement. She needed to see the face of the woman he wanted her to fight for. Gabe set down his cup and crossed to the row of gray metal filing cabinets along the east side of his office. Without being asked, Olivia followed him to the top left drawer. "Here." He pulled out the framed photo that had once sat on the corner of his desk and handed it to her. "This was our engagement picture, taken about five months before Dani died."

"She's beautiful," Olivia whispered on a sigh that was almost reverent.

The kindness of hearing someone else mourn the tragedy of Dani's death soothed the wounds inside him. But just when he should have been remembering the sweet vanilla scent that had been Dani's, his nose filled with the citrusy freshness emanating from Olivia's short hair. There was something electric about this woman, an excitement at noticing the feminine details behind the gun and badge, an anticipation of trading words and opinions—an unexpected jolt of purely male interest that hit him every time they were together. The visceral impact of these encounters which heated his blood and stirred things behind his zipper reminded Gabe that he'd moved beyond the grief he'd felt with Dani's death.

But he curled his fingers into a fist behind Olivia's back and dropped it to his side before he gave in to the impulse to touch that sable-colored hair. His grief might have abated, but the guilt sure as hell was still there. "Yeah. She was."

Olivia touched a fingertip to the glass. "Is this the engagement ring that was stolen?"

He nodded, forcing himself to forget the untimely attraction and remain as focused on the investigation as she was. "That, some gold hoop earrings and a wristwatch from a discount store."

"Was the jewelry expensive?"

"Not enough to give the Rockefellers a run for their money, but probably enough to feed a junkie's fix for a few weeks." Gabe plucked the picture from Olivia's fingers to put it back in its drawer. "I know what you're thinking—Dani wasn't murdered for the diamond she was wearing—"

"I have to consider every possibility."

Gabe closed the drawer. "You only have to consider the right one."

"The right one?" Olivia planted her hands at her hips and tipped her face to his. "Just because it's *your* theory, that makes it right?"

He mirrored her stance, watching the green fire of temper take over the color in her eyes. "Factually, I know you have to explore every possible motive and suspect— but what do you think I've been doing for six years? Your father and his partner never found the thief they were looking for because he didn't exist. Dani was killed to cover up a story."

"That's only one possibility. I have to revisit and rule out any other—"

A soft knock and the door opening ended the argument. A platinum blonde, wearing a designer suit that cost as much as his monthly salary, entered with a friendly smile that faded when she saw the two of them together. "Gabe, I… Sorry. Didn't know you had company." Gabe's boss, the slightly older woman who'd inherited the newspaper, but earned her CEO status and his respect with her business and management skills, tucked the small box she carried under one arm and walked right up to Olivia. "Hi. I'm Mara Boyd, publisher of the *Journal*."

The two women shook hands. "Detective Olivia Watson."

"Detective? Has something happened?" Mara tipped her bright blue eyes to his. "Has there been a break on Dani's murder? You know I want that story. She was our girl. Nobody gets to scoop us. Will you be able to write it? You deserve to have that vindication, but if it'll be too much, I'll assign it to someone else."

Olivia stepped in front of him, as though she meant to protect him from the verbal barrage. "Let's solve it first."

"Of course." Mara's gaze dropped back to Olivia. "But you being here is good news, right?"

"I hope so."

"Yes." Gabe closed his hands around Olivia's shoulders and scooted her to the side. He could fight his own battles. Not that talking business with Mara—or even something so personal as Dani's murder—was ever an issue. "Detective Watson is exploring the possibility of a link between Dani's murder and a death that occurred yesterday."

"Are you talking about Ron Kober's murder?" Mara asked.

Olivia subtly pulled away from the grasp of his fingers. "Did you know Mr. Kober?"

"Of course." Mara hugged the box she was carrying in front of her. "Ron delivered all kinds of press releases when he worked for Senator McCoy. I've met him at fund-raisers, and the paper did an article on him when he built the Kober Building and opened his private PR firm."

"Do you know of any dealings he might have had with Danielle Reese?" Olivia pressed.

"Dani and Ron?" Mara shook her head. "Dani was a cub reporter. They ran in different social circles. She wouldn't have been covering anything he was involved with."

Great. Just what Gabe didn't need—his boss contradicting his assertion that Dani and Kober had been working together. He stepped away from Olivia and escorted Mara back to the door. "Did you need something?"

Mara's smile was back. "I just wanted to remind you that you're covering the mayor's cocktail reception for party members and the press at the art gallery tomorrow night. And give you this." She placed the small, narrow box in his hands. "I didn't know if you had one of your own. I rarely see you wear them."

Gabe lifted the lid and arched an eyebrow at the black silk. "A tie?"

"I reserved the tux that goes with it at the rental place on the card inside. Plus, it's an election year, so you know there'll be a photo op. Madam Mayor may even be looking for our endorsement, but I'd like to hear her answers to some hard questions before I put the *Journal*'s name behind her. You know I'd go myself but, um…"

"I'll be there." Gabe knew firsthand about his boss's recent reticence to attend anything resembling a public society event. "I may even wear the stupid bow tie. Thanks."

"You're welcome. Keep me in the loop on any new developments with Dani's murder." Mara's smile included Olivia. "I'll let you two get back to work."

Gabe closed the door and tossed the tie box on top of his desk. "Where were we?"

Oh, right. Sniffing Olivia's hair, failing to keep his hands to himself, verbally duking it out with her and enjoying it all more than he should, considering Olivia represented the enemy he had to bring over to his side of the investigation.

"Your boss likes you."

"Because she knows I'll give her an honest opinion about what's really going on behind the mayor's party line."

"No, I mean she *likes* you." Olivia picked up her

coffee and drank a couple of swallows, using the cup to mask her assessment of his reaction.

She wasn't getting one. "The woman gave me a tie, not the key to her apartment."

"Have you two gone out?"

"We're friends. A couple of times she's needed an escort and I've obliged her so she doesn't have to mess with the whole dating-after-forty scene."

Olivia's eyes widened with mock surprise. "You date?"

Gabe circled around his desk opposite her. "Not every woman finds me to be—how did you put it?—*too damn arrogant* to spend time with."

When she lowered her cup, he was surprised to see that the cop could blush. "You *do* pay attention to details, don't you. Still, in the interest of the investigation, Ms. Boyd wouldn't happen to have a jealous streak, would she?"

He turned his chair toward her and sat. "Jealous of Dani? Mara hired her."

"To write for her newspaper—not to marry her star reporter."

Gabe considered the possibility for about two seconds, then shook his head. "Mara was married when I was with Dani."

"Some women want their cake…and everybody else's."

That wasn't the boss he knew. "I don't think so. Mara didn't have a good marriage. Her husband was Brian Elliot."

"The Rose Red Rapist?" Olivia's eyes widened at the mention of the serial rapist the department had put away a couple years earlier. Although, in Gabe's way of thinking, it had taken them far too long and far too many victims to identify Elliot and make the arrest.

"One and the same. Mara knew he wasn't right in the head, and shut down her feelings long before she got divorced. There was never any jealousy there. No strong emotion of any kind. The only thing she feels a passion for is this paper." Olivia set her coffee on the edge of the desk and started typing on her phone again. "You're not putting her down as a suspect, are you? Mara doesn't have it in her to kill anybody."

"But she'd have the money to hire someone to do it for her."

He pushed to his feet. "Olivia—"

"Fine. I'll move her to the bottom of my list."

"This isn't about jealousy." Gabe poked the desktop with each and every point. "We should be talking to Leland Asher. Or even Adrian McCoy and his people. We should find out if there was any recent contact between the three of them."

"*We* aren't going to do anything." Olivia lowered her phone, moving a step closer with every reply. "I'm the cop. I contact persons of interest and ask the questions."

"I'm a part of this investigation."

"You're going caveman on me again."

"Cave…" Gabe scrubbed his palm over his face and looked away, swearing at the apt description he'd given himself last night. But he wasn't about to back down from what he knew was right. He tapped his finger against his temple and settled back into his chair. "You need what I have in here to solve the case."

"Then how about a little information from that head of yours? Do you still have the story Dani was writing? Copies of her notes? Those would be more helpful than arguing with you."

Gabe clicked the mouse to bring icons back on his computer screen. "Dani kept her stories on a flash drive that she carried on her key chain. Had it with her all the time. I never saw what was on it." Olivia searched her phone again, while he brought up the different files of research he'd put together. "She made a few notes on her desk calendar—dates, times, code names—that I scanned. She called the source she was meeting with—"

"The source you believe to be Ron Kober?"

"Yes. She called him BB. Big Break. As in big break on the story she was writing—"

"Or the big break in her career." She held up her phone, although he couldn't read the text. "There was no flash drive collected as evidence. And her keys were still in the car at the scene. Do you still have it?"

"No. That proves somebody took it." Adrenaline rushed through Gabe's blood the same way it did when he broke a story. "You find out who has that flash drive and you'll have your killer."

"All it means is that we haven't found it yet. I texted a couple of detectives I work with who are at the impound lot to tear her car apart and see if she hid a flash drive somewhere that the crime scene techs never discovered." Olivia moved in beside him, reading the screen over his shoulder. "It also means I have to rely on you to tell me what was on that flash drive."

One step forward and two steps back. Gabe tempered his hope at finally getting through to KCPD with a good dose of cynicism. "Over the years, I've recreated as much of what I could remember from the notes Dani kept."

"But you don't have any of the actual notes or the article she was writing?"

"When we argued that night, she downloaded all the

files I'd read onto her flash drive and deleted them from her laptop."

Gabe felt Olivia's hand on the back of his chair. "Do you still have the laptop? Our tech guys can recover all kinds of data, sometimes even from corrupted files."

"She took it with her. Accused me of spying on her, not believing in her. Said she wasn't going to be treated like a rookie reporter anymore."

When the detective didn't immediately berate him for not having actual admissible evidence to share, he sought out her reflection on the monitor beside him. "That's a lot of guilt to carry with you, isn't it?" He watched her force the wistfulness from her expression before she patted his shoulder. "I'm sure the two of you would have made up, maybe even traded a laugh or a kiss, if she'd come back home that night."

Gabe reached up to capture her hand. The eyes weren't the only mystery he had yet to solve about this woman. "Sounds as though you know about that kind of guilt. What happened?"

But the quiet moment of a shared understanding didn't last. "What I know is that cold cases rely on plenty of circumstantial evidence to make a conviction. But so far all I have are bad guys with alibis, a missing flash drive and a lot of hearsay from you. A few tangible facts wouldn't hurt."

"So you get to ask questions, but I don't?"

Apparently not. Olivia pulled away with a determined huff and moved around the room, inspecting his office. Allowing his curiosity to simmer, he went back to pulling up files on the computer. "Did you know I was Thomas Watson's daughter when we met yesterday?" she asked. "Is that why you requested Jim and me from the Cold Case Squad?"

Gabe glanced up to find her oddly fascinated with a Missouri Press Corps certificate framed on the wall. "Not at first. I called Chief Taylor and made the request when I heard about Kober's murder. I didn't know he'd be sending you."

"Do you want someone else running this investigation?"

"Will you solve it?" he challenged. "Will you find Dani's killer?"

Her shoulders stiffened and her chin came up before she turned. Her eyes, all green and gold now, locked onto his as she came back to sit on the edge of the desk beside him, facing him. "Yes."

As much as her confidence intrigued him, six years was a long time to wait for the action and satisfaction he'd yet to see. "Do we bet money on this now, or what?"

"No bets. Just a promise that I'm going to do my job." His sarcasm hadn't fazed her a bit. She was dead serious, expecting him to take her at her word. "My father would have eventually solved the case, too, if he hadn't been injured and forced to retire. It always troubled him— haunted him, even—that he never found Dani's killer."

"Not as much as it has haunted me." But there was more regret than sneer in his tone. If he hadn't been such a self-righteous jerk back then, warning Dani she was going to crash and burn with her story—that she was playing way out of her league—she might still be alive. If only he'd done more than preach at her that night. If only he'd stopped her. Gone with her. Done anything besides let her go off and confront a killer alone. He needed to change the subject. "How did your father get injured?"

"High-speed car chase. His partner lost control of the car and they ran off the road." Finally, a question she would answer for him—although, interestingly, the question hadn't been about her. "They were both lucky they survived the wreck, but at the time, Dad was more worried about whether or not the perp got away."

"Did he?"

"No. He got caught in the accident, too. He's serving his sentence in Jefferson City." She moved some papers and brushed the dust off a trophy on top of the filing cabinets. "Dad and Al solved a lot of cases together, but neither one could return to regular duty after that. Dad works as a consultant for a security company now, but he hated having to retire from KCPD with an unsolved case."

"Dani's."

Olivia nodded.

"Is that why you're doing this? To avenge your father? To complete his service record?"

"Maybe a little." She traced the plastic lid on her coffee before picking up the cup and finishing it off. "I'm doing this because solving crimes is the job I'm trained to do. The job I swore an oath to do to the best of my ability. I know you don't have any appreciation for cops, Gabe. But I do. I take a lot of pride in protecting Kansas City, a lot of pride in being a detective. I do it because Dani and her family—and you—deserve justice."

He tilted his gaze to hers in a hard stare, assessing her sincerity and ability to make good on her words. "This isn't merely a personal quest for me, either. I'm just as committed to finding the truth as you are. It's what a good reporter does."

Refusing to look away from the challenge in his eyes, she returned to his desk. "So, if we're done trading philosophies, I'd like to get back to work. I have a feeling the only way I'm going to earn your respect, and redeem your opinion of my father and the rest of the department, is to show you how we get the job done."

Gabe stood to face her. "My beef with KCPD doesn't include you, Olivia."

She tipped her chin to keep their gazes locked. "You disrespect the department, you disrespect me."

"Fair enough. Prove me wrong about KCPD."

She inched a step closer. "Prove me wrong about reporters."

The beginnings of a smile tugged at the corner of his mouth and Gabe nodded. Despite the glimpses of some secret vulnerability, he hadn't run up against anyone in the department who was tougher than this lady right here. Maybe she was already halfway toward earning that respect.

He pulled out his chair for her to sit. "You can read what I've pieced together from Dani's report, along with the snippets I retrieved from her calendar and notebook. Then you'll know what I know."

Shaking her head, she pulled up the first file. "I'll know what you *suspect*," she corrected. "I'm still going to need witness corroboration or some other kind of proof before I can make an arrest."

"Are you and I ever going to agree on anything, Detective?"

She picked up her empty cup and held it out to him. "I like coffee. Do you?"

Gabe gave in to the urge to laugh before snatching her cup and heading for the door. "Keep reading. I'll go get us another cup."

Chapter Six

Olivia shifted her Explorer into Park and killed the engine before looking past Gabe to assess the rusting, swaybacked shell of Morton & Sons Tile Works.

Despite the puffy white clouds in the late-afternoon sky overhead, there wasn't anything cheery about this derelict block of condemned buildings. The pediment above the front doors with 1903 carved into it was one of the few bits of the brick-and-mortar facade not crumbling away from the rusting iron and chewed-up timber structure underneath. Olivia could smell the river on the other side of the warehouse, smell the faint stink of garbage or something else rotten that she wasn't in real favor of identifying. Boarded-up windows that had been used for target practice, and a building code warning sticker beside the front doors completed the feeling of death and decay about the old storage facility. "I don't much like the look of this place in the daylight. I can't imagine your fiancée coming to this part of town in the middle of the night."

Gabe drummed his fingers against the top of the rolled-down window—the only outward indication that being on the same street, in front of the same abandoned warehouse where Danielle Reese's body had been found, bothered him. "This is a hell of a lonely place to die. I wonder how many times Dani came here to meet her informant before I realized what she was doing and warned her it was too dangerous. The only people who come to this neighborhood are gangbangers, druggies and the homeless. Any reputable businesses have closed or moved to a better location. If Leland Asher or one of his men found her here…" He shook his head and turned back to Olivia. "Even if there was someone around to see what happened, this isn't a neighborhood where people like to talk to the police."

Olivia agreed. The only witness statements had come from the men who'd checked out the abandoned car and found Dani's body on their way to work the next morning. There wasn't anybody around that she could see, although it was hard to shake the feeling that there were eyes on them right now.

Glancing around at the broken windows and shadowed doorways across the street from the warehouse, she half expected to see two glowing, Halloween-like eyes staring back at her. But there was no one, of course. Nothing but some bits of trash and clouds of dust blowing along the empty street. Just a few blocks away, similar historic structures had been saved and remodeled to become a shopping district, apartments and restaurants. But there was no kind of care or redemption like that here. "I'm sure this is hard for you. I'd be happy to take you to a restaurant or coffee shop to wait until I'm done here."

Gabe's blue eyes stopped their scan of the neighborhood. "I'm not leaving you in this place by yourself. The last woman I knew who came here—"

"I'm not Dani. I've been trained for working in a questionable environment, and I'm certain I'm carrying more weapons than she did. Besides, I'm not here to roust out any witnesses or trap a suspect. All I'm doing is walking through an old crime scene, trying to visualize what happened that night. I'm not worried." Even though the prickle of awareness at the nape of her neck tried to tell her otherwise.

"All Dani had was a can of pepper spray. She shouldn't have come to this place alone. I should have protected her."

"You tried. You offered her your experience and wisdom and she ignored it. Maybe she thought she had something to prove."

"To whom?"

"To you." Gabe's blue eyes darkened like cobalt and fixed on her. Olivia didn't shy away from her point. Could he really not see the similarities here? "You seem to bring that out in people. You demand a high standard of excellence. Do the job now. Do it right. No mistakes allowed. If someone wants the mighty Gabe Knight's approval, then he or she has to go above and beyond normal expectations."

His drumming fingers stilled and tightened into a fist. "Am I really such a bastard?"

Pinching her thumb and forefinger together in the air between them, Olivia winked. "Little bit."

A low-pitched laugh rumbled through his chest, softening the hard lines of his face and alleviating some of the tension between them. "I'll try to work on that."

The rare gift of his laughter made her smile. "No, you won't."

"Probably not." The laughter ended on a resolute sigh as Gabe pushed open the car door and climbed out. "Come on. Let's get this over with."

Olivia grabbed the manila envelope from the seat behind her and got out of the Explorer. She made a sweep of their surroundings, still looking for those hidden eyes, before crossing the street and joining him on the sidewalk in front of the old Tile Works building. "Would you feel better if I called for backup?"

"Tremendously," he admitted in that sardonic grinching of his. "But we're here, and I don't want to be any longer than we have to." He, too, seemed to be scanning the area for any signs of life besides them. "What exactly are you looking for?"

She opened the envelope to pull out the pictures from six years ago, along with her father's crime scene report, making a point to keep the most graphic photos at the bottom of the pile where Gabe wouldn't see his fiancée's body or the pool of blood beneath it. "I want to re-create what we know about the crime. Visualizing what went down here may give us a clearer direction with our investigation. If we understand the how, then the why and the who might become more apparent."

Gabe held the envelope while Olivia lined up the images with their current surroundings. "Not much has changed except for the crime scene tape." Looking over her shoulder, he pointed to the rusted hinges on the front doors. "Other than that new padlock, it looks as though this place hasn't been disturbed in six years."

Olivia nodded, matching the double iron doors of the warehouse entrance with the background of the photo. He was right. There was no padlock back then. "Dani's car was parked against the curb here, and she was found on the sidewalk beside it, hidden from view from the street. There weren't any signs of a struggle inside the car, and no blood there, so she was already outside when she was shot. Probably talking to her informant, BB, someone she expected to see, someone she trusted enough to get out to talk to in this neighborhood in the middle of the night."

Gabe looked up and down the street. "There are plenty of places where her assailant could have hidden. Parked in a car in that alley. Up in one of those office buildings or warehouses across the street. He probably waited until her contact had left and ambushed her."

"If this was a carjacking, she'd have gotten out on the driver's side. I'm ruling that out." Olivia switched photos and knelt down where Dani Reese's body had lain, wondering why the woman would be trying to get into the passenger side of her car—or if there was some other reason why that door, instead of the driver's side, was open. She touched the spots on her back and chest where Dani had been shot. Once in the back when the shooter had surprised her, or she was running away. Once in the chest when he'd caught up to her. That shot had brought her down. "Even at night, she probably saw her shooter." Sinking back onto her haunches, Olivia looked up from the sidewalk where Dani had fallen, imagining a blank face where the killer would have stood over her. "With the small caliber of bullets that were used, he'd have to be fairly close."

When she touched her fingers to her face to note the kill shot, Gabe grabbed her hand, pulling it away. "Don't do that. Please."

With little more than a flare of his nostrils to reveal the emotions that must be reeling inside him at this re-enactment, Olivia switched her grip to squeeze his hand as she stood. "Sorry. Do you want to wait in the car?"

"Nope. Too far away." Gabe's grip tightened around hers before releasing her. "I want answers. But I'm not going to lose anyone else trying to find them. Understood?"

She reached up, obeying an impulse before really thinking it through, and brushed her fingertips along the firm line of his jaw. "I'll make it as quick as I can," she promised.

"Don't worry about me. I'm a crusty old bastard, remember? Just keep working. I'll be fine." He turned his face, tickling her fingers with a brush of soft stubble before pressing a quick kiss to her palm. "What's next?"

Little frissons of warmth tingled through the sensitive nerve-endings on her hand and she pulled away. It was just a thank-you kiss, an appreciation for the comfort she'd offered. It didn't mean anything more than that. There was no bond forming here.

With her brain misfiring on hormones and compassion, Olivia pulled up the next picture and forced herself to think about the murder. She looked at the picture in her hand, then down at the sidewalk where a few sturdy weeds were already turning green between the cracks.

There was one other difference in these photographs.

A different sort of electricity fired through her veins. She took two steps, three, four, away from the spot where Dani had died. Time and the elements had washed them away, but in the picture there were two tiny sprays of cast-off blood droplets, each one no bigger than a broccoli floret. Too small and too far away from the body to have come from the gunshots.

"Olivia?"

A six-year-old incident was starting to fall into place.

She went back to the curb where Dani's car had been parked and walked through what she was pretty certain had occurred that night. "Dani didn't open the passenger-side door that night. The killer did."

Gabe followed her path. "Why?"

She mimicked reaching inside the car. "To check the glove compartment. He was searching for something."

"The flash drive."

"Or proof of death. Sometimes with a hit, the killer has to bring the victim's ID to whoever hired him to prove the job is done." Gabe backed away when she turned and looked down at her feet, imagining Danielle Reese and a growing pool of blood there. "Our guy wasn't an experienced killer. He didn't want to touch the body if he didn't have to. That's why he shot her in the back first—from a distance. But he couldn't find what he needed in the car, so he went through her purse." She pulled out the previous photo. Dani's bag had a long strap that she wore across her body, from one shoulder to the opposite hip. Olivia knelt down, imagining how a man, anxious to get away as quickly as possible, would have gotten into the purse that was anchored beneath his victim. "He couldn't have pulled Dani's purse off her shoulder unless he moved her. That may have given him the idea to make it look like a robbery, if that wasn't his instruction in the first place."

She pretended to tug at the purse on the ground and rifle through the contents. Then she removed imaginary jewelry and stood. She stepped over the space where Dani had lain and walked toward the errant blood drops. Holding up her hand, Olivia looked at fingers that would have been wet with blood. "The report said this was Dani's blood, but she wasn't shot over here." She made the movements of flicking her hand. Twice. "He got blood on him, and it was freaking him out." Olivia lifted her gaze to the iron doors. "She didn't go into that warehouse. He did."

Gabe pointed to one of the photos he still held. "There was no padlock on the door six years ago." Olivia nodded and hurried back to her car. Gabe jogged behind her. "What are we doing?"

"Going inside that warehouse." She opened the back and put the photos inside before pulling the toolbox her father insisted she carry to the rear bumper. Between the clank of the tools shifting in the metal box and the drumbeat of anticipation pounding in her ears at the potential new lead on the case, Olivia hadn't been as alert to her surroundings as she should have been. But in the next moment of silence, she detected a low humming noise—like the sound of a car or machine engine idling in the distance. Olivia turned her head to the nearby cross street. "Do you hear that?"

"The traffic?" Gabe had turned to scan the abandoned buildings up and down the street the moment she did. Olivia tuned in to the stop-and-go sounds of vehicles in a residential area just a few blocks to the south. "There still may be some sump pumps working in the area since we're so close to the water."

"No, it's…" With a cooling breeze stirring up the hint of an evening rain shower, she was also more aware of the whoosh of the Missouri River current on the north side of the buildings as the water slapped against rocks on the shore and the pylons of old loading docks. She couldn't hear the sound of the engine at all, anymore. Maybe she'd imagined it. Or maybe, as Gabe had suggested, the sound had simply moved on with the flow of traffic. "It's nothing."

Time to scrap that fanciful flight of imagination. The watching eyes hadn't been there, either. She must still be a little off her game since that night when Marcus's infidelity made her question whether or not she could trust her own judgment. But she wasn't about to let Gabe

Knight see any hint of incompetence while she was on the job.

With a renewed sense of focus, Olivia handed Gabe a pry bar and pulled out a flashlight for herself. "Here, caveman. Make yourself useful."

"Really?" he mocked, dutifully taking the pry bar and closing the hatch for her. "Is that going to be a thing?"

"Well, there are other names I could call you," she teased right back. Joining in his low-pitched laughter, Olivia locked the Explorer and crossed the street to the iron doors of the Tile Works.

The steel padlock didn't immediately budge for Gabe, but with an extra oomph of muscle and a screeching surrender, the rusted bolts holding the hasp in place snapped in two. Olivia pulled at the outer door, but ended up having to put her shoulder into it and accept Gabe's help there, as well. The iron door itself was heavy, the hinges were rusty, and with the slight caving of the exterior wall, the tendency for it to swing shut again made it feel like pushing a dead car up a hill.

"I bet that hasn't been opened in six years." Olivia brushed the grime and dust off her hands and jacket before stepping inside the cavernous interior and turning on her flashlight. The sudden beam of light chased a band of small rodents and big bugs back into the shadows. "I love what they've done with the place."

"Wait. Unless you're going to arrest me for vandalism?" Olivia shook her head as Gabe pried off a piece of the framing from the inside of the door. It snapped off easily, indicating the wood was dry and rotten. "I don't think I'd lean against anything," Gabe warned, wedging the one-by-one between the door and the frame to prop it open. "I doubt it would hold up." Then he stood beside her, pulling back the front of his tweed jacket and propping his hands on his hips, heedless of the transfer of dirt and rust to his jeans. "Talk about a needle in a haystack. How do we find something the size of my little finger in here?"

"You mean the flash drive?" She swung her light up to the cobwebs hanging like Spanish moss from the second-story catwalk and stair railings, and the triangular ceiling joists holding up most of the roof. "I'm not sure what we're looking for. Hopefully, something here will tell us why the killer came in. Or better yet, who the killer is."

Gabe nodded beside her. "So where do we start?"

Windows on both levels had been boarded up. Some of the glass was intact, some had been broken by vandals using them for target practice, some had receded from their desiccated putty and fallen from their frames to shatter into dusty bits of shine on the concrete floor. The weight of a giant iron hook and heavy chains hanging from a winch near the dockside doors had pulled support timbers from the roof and peeled open several holes in the corrugated metal overhead. The openings in the roof let in enough sunlight to reflect off the dust motes floating through the stale air, and cast the interior in dim shadows. Olivia swung her light around at ground level, the extra illumination transforming hulking blobs in the corners into piles of wood pallets and cube-shaped stacks of old boxes.

"We start closest to the door. If our perp came in here to hide, he'd be looking for the first spot he could find." They went to the first pallet, where several rows of dust-shrouded cardboard boxes were stacked like bricks.

Gabe wiped off the top layer of dust to reveal the faded blue logo of Morton & Sons Tile. He lifted a box from the top to get a closer look, but the cardboard collapsed in his hands. He held it away from his body as sand and chips of broken tiles poured out onto the floor, sending a fresh plume of dust into the air that they both had to turn their eyes and noses from. Once the box was empty, he tossed it onto the pile of tile and grit. "Looks like old stock left over from when Morton & Sons went out of business. Age and moisture have turned the clay back to dust."

"Gabe." Olivia's attention had already moved on to the next pallet. Although the second stack of tiles was as perfectly cube shaped as the first one, something was out of place. "Look at that. Everything else is symmetrical here. Why is there an extra box sitting on top?"

Reaching over the top of the stack beside her, Gabe touched his fingers to a depression there. "This looks like a sinkhole. The boxes underneath must be caving in."

"Why?" she whispered, feeling that spark of anticipation again. She was on the verge of finding answers.

The urgency in Gabe's voice meant he could sense it, too. "Because there's an empty space beneath it."

"Where that box used to be." Retreating a step, Olivia ran her light over the stack again, stopping at a box three down from the top, about waist-high for her. "It's backward. The logo doesn't match up with the rest of the boxes in this stack." An idea, just as clear as a crime scene marker, flashed through her head. "Hold this."

After handing off the flashlight, she snapped a picture of the boxes with her phone. Then she hunched down to work her fingers into the seams between the boxes and pull the backward one out of the pile, as though removing a plank from a Jenga puzzle. Only, she was certain whatever she was about to find wasn't any game.

She waited for a line of sandy grit to stop spilling through the seam in the bottom before turning the box around. "Look."

Faint brown spots, five in the pattern of fingertips gripping the box to pull it from the stack, peeked out beneath the layers of dust.

"Is that blood?"

Olivia nodded and set the remnants of the box on top, snapping another photo. "I'll take that to the lab for analysis."

"So our killer who couldn't get Dani's blood off his hand pulled that box out. Why?"

"Your sink hole." Olivia tugged the sleeves of her jacket and blouse up her arm and flexed her fingers at the opening. "If anything in the rodent family runs up my arm, I *will* be screaming, and I'll have to shoot you if you tell anyone."

Gabe moved behind her to shine the flashlight into the empty cavity. "Good to know you have a weakness, Detective. Your secret's safe with me."

Slowly, she thrust her hand into the void. Up to her wrist. Up to her elbow. She stretched her fingers, hoping she'd find anything except a clump of fur and a worm-like tail. "You're sure it won't show up on the front page of the *Journal?* Do you have any idea how many mice and creepy-crawly things three brothers can find and bring into the—"

The iron door slammed shut and Olivia yelped. She jerked her hand back as if she'd been bitten.

"Easy." Gabe's firm hand closed over her shoulder, steadying her as the light in the warehouse dimmed and he looked across to the doors. "I don't think a rat did that. I wasn't sure that wood was going to hold, anyway.

Do you want me to find something sturdier to prop the door open with?"

"That's okay. There's still enough light in here."

The warmth of Gabe's hand remained on her shoulder as she reached inside the empty cavity again. But her startled heart rate didn't seem to be slowing any as her fingertips brushed against stiff, nubby material. "I've got something." She stretched half an inch farther and felt several hard, small items poke her through the dusty cloth. "If I could just reach… Got it."

Olivia closed her fingertips around a bunch of long threads and pulled out the hidden treasure. The threads turned out to be the fringe on a long green scarf. A cloud of dust stung her eyes and made them water when it plopped into her hand. She coughed the irritation from her throat and set the wad of material on top of the boxes to unfold it. "Is this Dani's?"

Gabe's shoulder brushed against hers as he moved in beside her to shine the light on their newly discovered treasure. "She liked to wear scarves. And I know she had one on that night. But I couldn't say for sure."

Olivia tugged at the material, stiff with mold and damp clay, untying several knots. "There's something tied up inside."

The flashlight beam wavered. "Did you hear that?"

She hadn't heard a thing beyond the rattle of whatever was inside the scarf clinking together. "Probably the building settling or some critter I don't want to know about running up the stairs." She blew a cloud of dust off the material and coughed again. "I need the light."

Gabe's focus was on their prize again. "Looks like more blood."

"The killer probably wiped his hands on it before stashing it in its hiding place." Olivia hesitated, glancing up at the grim shadows on Gabe's expression. "Maybe you shouldn't be here. I'm looking at things objectively, but it's all personal for you, isn't it?"

"I'm okay. Open it. I want to see what he took from her."

After loosening the last knot, Olivia flipped back the material. The light glinted off the sparkle of diamond facets and polished gold.

Gabe swore a guttural curse. "That's the ring I gave Dani."

"I recognize it from the photo." She pushed his hand away when he reached for the marquise solitaire. "I'm sorry. In case there's any kind of print or DNA left on it."

He shrugged off her sympathy. "What else is there?"

She took one more picture before pulling an ink pen from her pocket to scoot aside the other items that had been bundled up for six years. "Earrings and a watch. No sign of a billfold or ID." His gasp of hope deflated along with her own. "And no flash drive. I suppose that would be too easy. Wait a sec." Gripping the pen between her fingers, she stuck her arm back inside the opening, extending her reach. "I felt something else in there."

"Olivia?" The wary suspicion in Gabe's tone barely registered as her pen tapped against something hard.

With her cheek smooshed against the dusty boxes, she could barely hear him, anyway. "Maybe it's just a broken tile. I can touch it, but I can't grab it. Wait a minute. That's metal on metal. What if that's a gun? It could be the murder weapon." This cold case was heating up. But not if she couldn't retrieve the evidence. She pulled her hand back out. She slid the scarf to one side and lifted the box on top. "I'm going to have to dig it out."

"Olivia!"

She looked up at his sharp tone. Looked beyond him to the front doors where the beam of the flashlight danced off a gray, swirling haze that grew thicker by the second. "What is that?"

"Smoke."

Chapter Seven

A bright ball of flame bloomed at the base of the old timber beam beside the front door as though a giant matchstick had just been struck. The fire ebbed in its initial intensity, but the shower of sparks drifting through the smoke found purchase on the rotted wood. Each glowing ember ignited a tiny new fire of its own. In a matter of seconds, the flames branched out along the crosspieces above the door frame and climbed any available path toward the ceiling.

"We need to go," Gabe urged.

Olivia wrapped up the scarf and its contents and zipped it inside her jacket. The more the fire consumed, the brighter it burned and the faster it seemed to spread. But she wasn't going anywhere without that gun, if that was, indeed, what she suspected was hidden inside. She flipped the top box off the pallet and reached for the next one. "I need to retrieve everything in here."

Gabe's hand clamped over her arm, pulling her away. He thrust his arm inside the collapsing stack and pulled out the small caliber weapon along with a snowy cascade of dust and grit. "Ah, hell. Do you think this...?"

He didn't need to finish that choked-off question. Yes. Chances were that was the gun that had killed his fiancée.

Olivia plucked the small semiautomatic from his hand and stuffed it into the back of her belt. With flames shooting up to the second story now, there wasn't time to worry about trading compassion or compromising potential evidence. She grabbed the box with the bloody fingerprints and tucked it beneath her arm. "We need to go *now*."

With a curt nod, Gabe fell into stride beside her and they ran to the iron doors. By the time they reached them, she'd dialed 9-1-1.

"This is Detective Olivia Watson. I'm reporting a structure fire at the old Morton & Sons Tile Works on—"

"Wait!" Gabe shot his arm out in front of her and stopped her from touching the iron door. He held his hand out about five inches from their only unlocked, unbarricaded exit before quickly snatching it back. Then he leaned forward and spit on the door. Even through the mask of smoke, she could hear the moisture sizzling on the hot iron surface and they both retreated. "It's too hot. We need to find another way out."

"We must have created a spark when the door slammed shut."

"I don't think so." He nudged the one-by-one on the floor with his shoe. It had a swirl of char marks at one end while the rest of the wood glowed like an ember and was turning to ash. "That's a pour pattern from an accelerant. I saw that at a trio of arson fires I covered a few years back."

"This was deliberate? Why? A stupid prank? Do you think they knew we were in here?" Olivia blinked at the gritty air irritating her eyes and sinuses, and followed the swing of Gabe's flashlight as he searched for another exit. She finished her call to Dispatch, warning them of the two people inside and possible arson before giving up on escaping through the fire and smoke and scalding temperature at the front doors.

"We answer questions later, Liv. Come on." Gabe slapped his hand into hers and pulled her into a run beside him. The flames seemed to chase them across the ceiling joists overhead. When they reached the back iron doors that opened onto the loading dock and river below, he released her hand, tossed her the flashlight and pulled the pry bar from the rear pocket of his jeans. He wedged the tip between the double iron doors.

But even with Olivia setting down the box and pushing her shoulder to the door, and Gabe putting his full weight on the pry bar, they couldn't open more than a crack between them. Matching guttural roars marked the physical exertion and frustration that could quickly give way to fear. A glimpse of shiny silver through the centimeter-wide opening gave them the bad news. "It's padlocked from the outside."

Gabe didn't waste time maneuvering to find an impossible angle to pop the hasp the way he had the front door. Instead, he hurried to the window at the right side of the door. With more shared muscle they pushed it open and attacked the boards nailed to the outside. But the splashes below warned them that this avenue of escape wasn't much more promising.

The exposed timbers behind them popped and crackled, cheering at the new source of oxygen they'd let in. Gabe started out the window, but dropped back to his feet. His mouth hung open as he fought to breathe in a gasp of fresh air. But his eyes were hard. "Can you swim?"

Brushing away the tears of irritation that dribbled over her cheeks, Olivia stuck her head out the window and looked straight down two stories to the river. The dock had been built up for boats to unload their goods, but the only thing below their position was a few feet of rocky bank and the muddy green of the Missouri. Full with spring rains falling upriver, the water eddied and swelled and blustered on past the dock pylons.

"Not that well. But I can try." She just prayed they missed the rocks, hit deep enough water and didn't get caught in any currents that would drown them before they ever made it to shore.

Olivia inhaled one breath, two, psyching herself up for the long, dangerous plunge. On the third breath, the toxic air scraped her throat and she coughed. "We have to…" She braced her hands on her knees as the coughing fit worsened. "We have to go," she wheezed.

"Easy." Gabe splayed a warm, soothing hand against her back. "We can do this."

"Of course I can do this."

"I didn't say *I*. I said *we*. We're a team now, remember?"

The massage and the urge to argue stopped at the yawing sound of metal heating and stretching. The noise skittered up her spine like the scurrying steps of unseen vermin scattered through the walls. Instinctively, Olivia moved closer to Gabe, curling her fingers into the lapel of his jacket as they both lifted their gaze. The crossbeams linking the outer walls were bowing. Flames crawled above their heads toward the heavy winch and hook anchored above them. That contraption could crush them or bring down the entire roof if it fell.

Gabe swore against her ear. "I know why they condemned this place."

But looking up had given Olivia an idea.

She pushed away, grabbing the box with the bloody

prints as she pointed the flashlight into the rafters. "Up there!"

Spotting the chipped red-and-white exit sign beside an oversize window on the catwalk level, they moved at a crouching run to the grated metal stairs and climbed toward the second-floor fire escape. Each step took them into heavier smoke and hotter air, making it more difficult to breathe and see. Each step made Olivia more and more aware of just how brittle this aging structure had become. The stairs shifted and sagged the higher they climbed, unused to any weight, and weakened by the rising temperature, perhaps.

Olivia's boot hit the next step and the whole stairwell lurched, taking a thirty-degree tilt to the right. Her leg slid from beneath her and she clutched at the left railing. She lost her grip on the box and flashlight and they plunged into the pallets burning below her. With her balance off-center, her palm slipped and she tumbled beneath the right railing toward the fiery abyss.

But the long, strong fingers of a sure hand clamped over her wrist, catching her as she fell over the side. "Olivia!"

Pain snapped through her shoulder and rib muscles at the abrupt stop to her momentum. Her jacket slid up her torso as she swung out, and the knotted scarf dropped from its cache and plummeted into the fire.

"The evidence!"

"Forget it! It doesn't do us any good if we don't get out of here. Grab on!" Gabe shouted, his voice hoarse with smoke. "I've got you."

The ache in her side robbed her of breath but also renewed her will to escape and survive. When she swung back like a pendulum, she caught the edge of the stair with her right hand, curling her fingers through the grate and hanging on. With one hand on the left railing and his feet braced on the wonky stairs, Gabe pulled at her sore arm, lifting her inch by inch until she could latch on to the metal with both hands. He shifted his grasp to her belt and pulled her onto the stairs and onto her feet before pushing her up the last few steps to the catwalk.

"We're almost there," he gasped against her ear. With his hands on her waist, he was half lifting, half guiding her along the catwalk.

Although her vision was blurred and her breathing was shallow, Olivia could feel the metal vibrating beneath her feet. The strain of the broken steps pulling at it, combined with the heat making the metal expand, meant they had only minutes, seconds, perhaps, before the whole structure collapsed. "We have to hurry."

"I know. Stay put."

When he tried to lean her against the brick wall beside the window, she swatted his hands away. "I'm all right," she lied, clutching her arm to her side. She was light-headed and coughing again, and the wrench of muscles from that fall made every breath a sharp stab in her side. But she was damned if she was going to play the little woman needing to be rescued. She pulled the pry bar from Gabe's back pocket. "Just break the glass."

"Turn your head away," he warned, bringing the heavy metal tool back and smashing the window glass.

The building moaned, as if the new influx of oxygen was more than it could take. The catwalk trembled in earnest. Billowing black smoke snaked toward them and up through the holes in the roof, gathering like a storm cloud in the rafters because it couldn't get free quickly enough.

As Olivia broke off shards of glass at the base of the window, Gabe pried off one board, then two. After he'd shoved the third board off onto the top of the fire escape, he tossed the pry bar through the window and his hands were at her waist again. "Can you get through?"

With a nod and a boost, Olivia climbed onto the sash and crawled outside. Gabe's shoulders and chest were a tighter fit. She tugged at the next board and then at the collar of his jacket to help pull him through.

With Olivia on her rump and Gabe on his hands and knees atop the metal grating of the fire escape, they spared a few precious seconds to cough soot from their lungs and breathe in fresh air. But the smoke pouring out behind him was a reminder that they weren't out of danger yet.

"I'm sorry about losing the engagement ring and scarf," she apologized. "Even if we recover it later, the fire will have destroyed any DNA or trace. And that box with the fingerprints is already toast."

Gabe shook his head, pushing to his feet. "I don't care."

"I thought that was going to be our big break on the case." She patted the gun wedged behind her back. "At least I've still got this. And the pictures on my phone. We can go back in after the firefighters clear—"

"I said I don't care," he snapped at her. He thrust a sooty, grimy, nicked-up hand in front of her face. "This place took Dani from me. I'm not about to let it take you, too."

Olivia tilted her stinging eyes to his hard, unreadable gaze and let him pull her to her feet. "I'm not going anywhere."

As if a fire in an old deathtrap or his blunt opinions could make her quit this case.

The standoff ended with the warning pop of rivets separating the fire escape from the crumbling brickwork. They both turned their heads at the frighteningly familiar vibration of old metal battling to endure beneath unexpected weight and the forces of the infrastructure shifting on the other side of that wall.

They both swore a choice word and raced down to the first-floor platform. When they tried to release that ladder, though, it wouldn't budge. "Looks like it's been soldered together so trespassers won't climb on it." Olivia shook the stationary ladder in frustration, instantly regretting the flash of temper when it aggravated the pulled muscles in her side. She hugged her elbow to her ribs once more. "That's another twelve feet or more to the ground."

"It's not that far for me." Gabe wasted no time swinging his leg over the edge of the railing and hanging from the bottom rung of the ladder before dropping the last few feet to the sidewalk below. He stretched his arms up toward her. "Jump." Sparks sailed out the window above and drifted through the air around them. Another bolt broke free of the mortar and the whole thing jerked. Olivia cried out, startled, but Gabe stood his ground beneath her. "I'm not going anywhere, either, Liv. You have to trust me."

"No, I don't." Going back into that fire would be easier than giving another man her blind trust. But little these past few months and days had been easy. "I hate when people say that," she muttered as she climbed over the edge of the railing. "Trust shouldn't be automatic—"

"Jump, Detective!" he ordered.

Bracing for the jolt through sore muscles, Olivia released her grip. She slammed into Gabe's chest, knocking him off his feet. Strong arms circled around her as they tumbled to the ground. A sheltering hand cradled her head against his neck as the impact jolted through both of them, and they rolled several feet to avoid the chips of brick and mortar pinging down around them.

Gabe and Olivia came to a stop in a side lot, lying side by side, their legs tangled together, her arms clutched between them. By unspoken mutual consent, they each exhaled an exhausted breath and lay there for several seconds without moving.

Olivia appreciated the cool surface of the shaded concrete more than she expected, and relished not having to come up with any more strength or resolve or courage for the moment. They lay there, beyond the reach of falling debris, long enough for all the aches and bruises on her battered body to register. The shallow, slowing puffs of Gabe's breath stirring her hair, along with the low-pitched rumble of laughter in his chest beneath her ear registered, too.

"Is every day always this exciting with you?" he wheezed against her ear, his sarcasm as evident as the muscular thigh wedged between hers.

Olivia's fingers tangled in the collar of his shirt and a breathless laugh of her own joined his. "I thought it was your fault."

Gabe's hold on her shifted and he rolled onto his back, bringing her halfway on top of him. "You are one tough lady, aren't you."

Olivia raised up on her elbow as his strong hands that had saved her more than once today framed her cheeks and jaw. She was ensnared by cobalt eyes that studied her face, then widened, as if he'd discovered her real secret.

Not so tough, Mr. Knight. Olivia brushed her fingers over the dark stubble above his mouth, wiping away the soot that clung there. She hadn't been held for a long time. She hadn't wanted a man to hold her since Marcus.

That this man who should be her enemy could make her want like this, could make her feel a little less like a cop and a little more like a woman...

As if hearing her unspoken thoughts, Gabe raised his head and touched his lips to hers in a tentative kiss. It was a simple meeting of one mouth touching another, testing the welcome, getting acquainted.

The second kiss was a little less gentle, a little more potent, a lot more purposeful in the way his fingertips tightened against her scalp and his tongue slipped between the seam of her lips to demand and find a response. A moan of something like satisfaction echoed in Gabe's chest and resonated within her own.

Olivia curled her grubby fingers into his collar and held on, matching each foray of his tongue, each caress of that hard, sensuous mouth. This kiss was a mix of *hooray, we made it,* and that undercurrent of electricity that had been buzzing between her and Gabe from the moment they'd met. She'd expected him to taste like the dark, hearty coffee she'd seen him drink, and that flavor of richness was there in the background. But his mouth was ashy from the smoke, hot from exertion and so leisurely thorough and gentle on her lips and tongue that Olivia was at once grateful for his patience and frustrated by the very same. She stretched herself against Gabe's muscled chest, urging him to deepen this exploratory kiss and unleash the desire she could sense he was holding back.

But this unplanned meeting of two wary hearts, exposed by the challenge of their very survival, didn't last.

The roar of a powerful engine revving up to speed tore Olivia's attention from the soulful heat of Gabe's embrace. The noise was a jarring reentry into the real world of bad guys and danger and knowing the handful of people she trusted in this world didn't include the man on the sidewalk beneath her. Olivia raised her eyes to the street in front of the warehouse and pushed away, her cop's training reacting when her own self-defense mechanism had shorted out.

Gabe, too, rolled to his hands and knees as she scrambled to her feet and ran toward the screech of rubber spinning across the pavement, screaming for traction as the vehicle made a sharp turn.

But the chase was short-lived. By the time Olivia reached the front of the burning warehouse, there was no adrenaline left to call on. Her legs wobbled with exhaustion, she was winded and that all-too-familiar car was nothing more than a black shadow disappearing around the corner. Olivia bent forward, bracing her hands on her knees as another coughing fit wracked her sore body. "Who are you, you son of a bitch?"

She could hear the sirens now, over the pulse hammering in her ears, and knew that help was on the way.

"Did you see that?" she asked Gabe, certain that was the same car that had followed her that morning. She hated that she'd missed getting a look at the driver again—hated that a stranger had the advantage of that kind of knowledge over her.

A blur of brown tweed and denim moved past her. "Black car. I only caught the taillights. He probably stopped to gawk at the fire."

"Did you get a license?" He gave no response, so she assumed that was a no. "Me, neither."

"Olivia."

She straightened at the grim tone of Gabe's voice and turned toward the warehouse. His attention had moved on to something besides a speeding car and an untimely kiss, as though neither of them mattered, and she forced herself to do the same.

Flakes of ash floated along with the glowing bits of wood and debris in the air like some devilish version of snowfall. Olivia raised her arm in front of her face to shield herself from the burning heat emanating from the building, and walked toward Gabe. He was standing in front of the double iron doors again. Well, as close as he could get with the ovenlike temperature coming off the warping metal. He snapped a picture with his phone.

"What is it?"

They both jumped at the loud crash inside as the heavy winch fell. The concrete shook beneath their feet. Flames shot through the roof. Windows shattered against their barricades and joined the debris raining down around them. Gabe backed them both across the street to stand behind her SUV, away from the fire. "I think somebody's trying to make a point."

If it wasn't made of brick or metal, it was burning now. The smoke and flames eating away at the building now made it difficult to see. But the picture on Gabe's phone was clear.

Sabotage.

Olivia's blood chilled despite the heat and she hugged her good arm over the one she had injured. Just as with the board Gabe had shown her inside, the charred black marks of an accelerant poured over the doors and sidewalk out front meant that this fire was no accident.

And whoever set it—the driver of that black car, perhaps—hadn't wanted them to come out alive.

GABE SAT ON the rear bumper of the ambulance, dutifully holding the oxygen mask to his nose and mouth while the paramedic cleaned and doctored the cuts on his hand. He'd sat here more than an hour now, watching the organized chaos of first responders and follow-up personnel.

Three fire engines had been called to the scene, along with two ambulances and enough black-and-white and unmarked police vehicles to line the block and two side streets. Either there was some historical significance to the roofless shell that had once been Morton & Sons Tile Works he didn't know about, Olivia was a relative or friend to half the department or they'd all come to see for themselves if KCPD Enemy #1, Gabriel Knight, had perished in the blaze.

He'd seen the looks, caught some snippets of gossip about the trash-talking reporter who thought he could do their job better. And what the hell was Thomas Watson's daughter doing with him, anyway?

The fire had been contained. The scene was secure. He'd been questioned by an arson investigator with an artificial leg, and had given a statement to both a uniformed officer and a detective. He'd even chatted with some reporters and photographers he knew from the *Journal* and other media outlets. Night had fallen and various headlights and spotlights added brightness and created shadows. And while there seemed to be just as many spectators as there were professionals on the scene, his attention remained focused on the short-haired detective with her left arm in a sling and her beautiful eyes fixed in an expression of weary patience.

He'd watched a buff, dark-haired cop pull up and try to start a conversation with Olivia. But her touch-me-not body language and the arrival of her father and two of her brothers had sent him away.

Although she'd reassured her family enough to convince them to leave, the other members of her cold case team remained on the scene. Olivia was leaning against her car now, maybe twenty yards from his position, close enough that he could make out parts of their conversation through the noise around him. A big blond guy who needed a shave, and an even bigger, clean-cut guy who ought to be playing the offensive line for the Chiefs, each gave her a brotherly squeeze on her good shoulder before apologizing about a car they'd searched being "Clean as a whistle." From the gist of the conversation, Gabe figured out that they were the ones who'd gone through Dani's car, looking for any sign of the missing flash drive.

A third detective in a suit and tie had brought his wife to the scene. Gabe's guess was that they'd been on a date or to some function—but they cared enough about Dani's murder—or the lead detective on the case, at any rate—to interrupt their evening and be here to check on Olivia and the new developments she'd found. And while his dark-haired wife waited at their pickup truck, chatting with friends she knew on the scene, the blond detective bagged the gun Gabe had pulled from the hiding place Olivia had found inside the warehouse. Now the man was jotting notes while she talked.

"I'm done, sir." A voice from right beside him interrupted Gabe's observations. Gabe pulled off his oxygen mask and the paramedic with the blue gloves handed him a card. "If you develop any of these secondary symptoms from smoke inhalation, get to an ER immediately. Otherwise, you're already on antibiotics that'll help these cuts, and your lungs and sinuses look clear. Just get some rest."

"Thanks." Gabe handed off the gear, pocketed the card and picked up his smoke-filled jacket before making a beeline for Olivia. He didn't like this distance between them, didn't like not knowing all the details her team was discussing about Dani's case, didn't like the protective impulses firing inside him each time she rubbed her temple or reaffixed that "I'm okay" smile on her face.

He no longer had any doubts that Olivia Watson was good at her job. She was as dedicated and smart as he'd want any cop to be. But he wondered if anyone else was aware of her fatigue, her pain or those glimpses of frustration and vulnerability that cowed her posture or flattened her smile for a split second when no one was looking. Maybe it was just his eye for detail that noticed those tiny chinks in her armor and wanted to make sure that no one took advantage of them. She was his strongest ally in solving Dani's murder, after all.

Plus, he was seeing a painfully familiar parallel between the dangers Dani had faced during her investigation and the two life-threatening events he'd been through with Olivia. Someone in Leland Asher's organization or on Senator McCoy's team, or a third party they had yet to uncover, was working very hard to keep old secrets buried. They'd killed a naively ambitious young reporter, and now they seemed to be targeting the sexy lady detective.

He had to finish Dani's story. He had to find the truth.

But he couldn't go through the pain of losing someone he felt responsible for twice. Whatever he could do, whatever the task required of him, he would see that Olivia didn't end up the same way Dani had.

As he approached Olivia's car, Gabe could make out more of the conversation with the cop in the suit. Olivia was giving him a vague description of the black car they'd seen speeding away after their escape. "I didn't get a good look at it. I have no idea if it's connected to the fire or even my investigation. But I've seen it before."

"Do you think the driver has been following you?"

"Possibly," she admitted. Gabe didn't like the sound of that. Had he put her in more danger than he thought?

"That's not a lot to go on, but I'll make it my first priority."

"Thanks, Jim."

The male detective put away his pen and paper. "You going to the hospital or home?"

"Home. The medics cleared me. I just need a long, hot shower."

Really? An image of those long, lean curves naked and glistening under a spray of steam and water should not be the first thing that popped to mind, given the seriousness of the conversation and Gabe's intent for joining them. The leap in his pulse and the interest stirring behind his zipper fought to keep hold of the wish he forced from his mind.

"Good. I'll call you as soon as I find out anything." The blond picked up the paper bag with the gun they'd recovered off the hood of Olivia's SUV. "I'll get this over to the lab." He waved an almost done to his wife before turning back to Olivia. "What about Knight? Have you had your fill of him? You want us to drive him home?"

Olivia's head turned, hearing Gabe's footsteps as he joined them on the sidewalk.

"Knight can take care of himself if Detective Watson needs to get home right away," Gabe announced. He didn't stop until he stood beside her, facing the male detective. "I saw the black car, too. Got a glimpse of it, anyway. It was a newer model. Six or eight cylinders under the hood, judging by the sound of the engine. Not manufacturer issue. Could have been a souped-up Charger or Challenger."

Olivia straightened away from the car, cradling her

arm in the sling, or maybe just hugging a protective shield around herself. "Gabe, this is my partner, Jim Parker. Gabriel Knight. He's a reporter with the *Journal*."

Detective Parker stepped forward to shake hands, his expression polite but wary. "I've read your articles."

"No doubt."

"Olivia? You want me to stay?" Her partner wasn't budging until she gave him the all clear. Good. She wasn't as alone against this chaos as he'd imagined her to be.

She shook her head. "I got it. Keep me posted on anything the lab says. Thanks, Jim."

"See you in the morning at roll call?"

Olivia nodded. Jim rejoined his wife in their pickup truck and drove away.

"Come on, caveman." Her gaze tipped up to his for a brief moment, revealing surprise, embarrassment and ultimately regret before she raised a placating hand and turned toward the car. "Sorry."

Okay, so it wasn't the most flattering nickname a woman could give him. Yet Gabe liked the fact that Olivia Watson wasn't afraid to say what she thought, right to his face instead of behind his back. He headed around the car while she fished her keys from the pocket of her soot-stained khakis. "It's okay. Blame it on the long day and let's get out of here." He nodded toward the sling she wore around her left arm. "Unless you want me to drive?"

"I don't need a man to drive my car for me."

But she was clearly exhausted. When she dropped her keys and muttered a curse, Gabe beat her to the curb to retrieve them from underneath the car. "Switch."

She arched an eyebrow at the order. "You do realize

there's not a cop on this block who isn't watching us right now."

"I know. Does that bother you?"

"Doesn't it bother you?"

"I call things as I see them. I understand there will be hard feelings with that kind of honesty."

With a reluctant sigh, she walked around to the passenger door. "Everything's black and white with you, isn't it? Right or wrong. Good or bad. That seems like a cold, lonely way to live."

She had no idea. "I'm not always right, Liv. I don't get my facts wrong. But sometimes, I make mistakes about people. I made a mistake about you. I'm sorry I judged you against the standard of any other cop."

"Like my dad?"

Ouch. So defending the family honor was working on her, too. Gabe absorbed the rightful pang of guilt and opened his door. But he didn't get in. This needed to be said. "I thought your dad and Junkert should have solved the case. I didn't know about his accident or how he felt about leaving the force with unfinished business. I'm coming at this from the victim's side when I've criticized the department for dragging its feet on an investigation. Finding answers and hearing someone take responsibility for the wrong they've done is all we have to make up in some small way for the loss we've suffered."

"You think we don't know that?"

Gabe tapped his fist on top of the car, torn between his loyalty to one woman and his concern for another. "I've always believed that victims and their families need a voice. And I'm the SOB who's going to stand up and be that voice."

Her eyes were a deep storm green in the shadows. "Most of the time, we do our job right. We get the bad guys off the street and the victims and their families thank us for it. Why don't you print any of that?"

Because he'd been eaten up by guilt and pain for so long that it was hard to put a positive, hopeful spin on things when he hadn't felt much of that positivity and hope. Until now. Until Ron Kober's murder offered them a lead. Until Olivia Watson took over the case. "I'm sure your dad tried to find Dani's killer. If he's got half the determination you do, I know he tried. I didn't fully understand how determined Leland Asher and Senator McCoy were about keeping their collusion a secret. But I do now. I'll try to keep a more open mind about the department."

"You really do have a way with words, don't you." Why didn't that sound like a compliment? Olivia tipped her chin up to a nearby streetlamp, stretching her long neck before meeting his gaze over the roof of the Explorer. "How do you feel about no words at all? I'll trade ten minutes of not talking about the fire, not talking about the case, not talking about my family—not talking about anything—for that ride back to your car."

He braced his forearms on the door frame and leaned toward her. "Olivia, you know what we need to talk about."

That kiss. The way her hand felt in his. This unexpected emotional connection. The hungry urge simmering beneath the surface to kiss her again. To do it right this time—not on a concrete slab, not when they both reeked of smoke and fatigue. Not when she was locked down so tightly that he could see the muscle pulsing along her jaw.

She was no dummy. The blush on her cheeks indicated that she knew exactly what he was referring to. But she shook her head adamantly and opened her door.

"Ten minutes, Gabe. Please. I need some time to sort through things and regroup."

In ten minutes, she'd be dropping him off and driving away. "So we catalogue what happened between us with your phobia of small rodents? We keep it a secret, or else?"

Her voice was an angry whisper over the roof of the car. "I won't threaten to shoot you because you kissed me."

"You kissed me back."

"Ten minutes, Gabe." Her temper dimmed as quickly as it had flared. "Or you're walking. Deal?"

He wasn't going to add to her stress. As long as they solved Dani's murder, it would be enough. It should be enough. But it didn't feel like finishing a long-overdue job and then walking away could ever be enough with this woman.

Still, he'd been driven and obsessed and shut off from his heart for so long, he wasn't used to feeling anything but grief or guilt or anger. He'd be foolish to think whatever emotions he was feeling tonight meant anything to her—meant anything at all. Maybe he needed those ten minutes, too.

Gabe waited until she was buckled in before climbing in beside her. "Deal."

Chapter Eight

"I heard you've been spending time with Gabe Knight from the paper." Duff Watson pushed open the door into the Fourth Precinct lobby and cleared a path for Olivia to enter without anyone jostling her sore arm.

Rolling her eyes at the attention her volunteer chauffeur was drawing to the black sling she wore over her short gray jacket, she walked past her oldest brother. "He's a consultant on a case I'm working on. Danielle Reese's murder."

"Dad's old case?"

She nodded, stopping in the middle of the marble-tiled foyer. "You were at the hospital. You saw that Gabe and Dad knew each other."

"Yeah, but I figured that was a one-time thing." Duff muttered something under his breath. "I didn't know you two were going to be joined at the hip. Keir said he was at the scene of the fire with you last night. That the two of you escaped together."

"He knows more about that case than anyone." Duff had been a detective longer than she had. He knew that made Gabe her primary lead. "I'm hoping to kill several birds with one stone—take a killer who's gotten away with murder for six years off the streets, get Dad that perfect record he wants—and Lieutenant Rafferty-

Taylor wants me to try to mend some fences between Gabe and the department. Get us some positive press."

Duff, a younger, taller ringer for their stocky father, stuffed his hands in his jeans and drew in a deep breath. Maybe he was feigning surprise, and maybe he was just using his big silhouette to shield her from the officers and staff filing through the lobby. "That's a tall order."

"He's doing his job, Duff. The same way we do ours."

He nodded to some friends he knew from the drug task force he was currently assigned to before facing her again. "Yeah, but Knight has a way of putting things that makes it sound like he's got a personal vendetta against the department."

"Danielle Reese was his fiancée."

"That's rough." Duff rubbed his hand at the back of his neck, conceding that much.

"I try to put myself in his shoes and understand where he's coming from by remembering how we felt when Mom was killed." Olivia's gaze dropped to the KCPD logo on her brother's jacket, the only outward sign she allowed for the pain she could so vividly remember. "I was either crying all the time or angry at everyone." She pushed aside the memories and looked up again. "I said and did some things I regret—until Dad and Uncle Al caught that dopehead, and the healing started."

"You were only nine years old, kiddo. We all lashed out back then. Knight's a grown man."

"That doesn't make it any easier. I was scared that guy was going to come after me or one of you guys or Grandpa until I saw him in handcuffs on his way to prison." She shrugged, then winced as renewed ache in her shoulder ligaments made her wish she hadn't. "I don't think Gabe has any family here to worry about. But he's got friends, and the people of Kansas City he's speaking for. Maybe he takes us to task because he's worried his fiancée's killer is going to hurt somebody else—or already has."

"Whose side are you on?"

Olivia blew out a frustrated puff of air that lifted her bangs. Her words had echoed the speech Gabe had given her last night. They had more in common than she would have ever guessed, but her brother wouldn't understand this growing affinity she was feeling for the reporter. She wasn't sure she understood it herself. "I'm not on anybody's side. I'm just stating facts."

Duff reached out with a gentle finger to poke the strawberry scrape on her cheekbone. "The only fact that I'm interested in is that you seem to keep getting hurt around Knight."

"Technically, he's getting hurt because he's hanging out with me."

"All I see is you in a sling, sportin' those bruises on your face." Duff's fingers went back to his pockets. "I'm glad Dad called me."

"He shouldn't have." Apparently, showing up at the scene of the fire and a report from the EMT last night hadn't been enough to ease her father's concern. She shouldn't have been surprised to find her big brother at her front door this morning, waiting to drive her to her appointment at the clinic. "I pulled some muscles— nothing major. The doctor said I didn't even have to wear this if I take it easy, and then, only for a couple of days. If it weren't for Gabe, I'd have been fried to a crisp yesterday. He saved me."

"Now you're defending him? If Dad could hear you—"

"If Dad was here right now, I'd tell him the same thing." Olivia did a little poking of her own, right in the middle of her brother's chest. "Gabe wasn't the bad guy yesterday. It took both of us, working together, to get out of that warehouse. Trust me, somebody didn't want us to."

The lines beside Duff's green eyes crinkled with a teasing grin. "You got a thing for this guy?"

"What?" Olivia groaned and pushed him on his way. One kiss after a close call did not make her and Gabe a *thing*.

"Seriously." He waved his hands in front of her face, pointing out her tone and expression. "You've got that whole mama bear defending her territory thing going on right now."

Sometimes she wondered who the mature sibling really was in this family. "Get back to work. I have to get upstairs to roll call."

This conversation had already lasted too long and gotten too personal. But the big galoot wouldn't take the hint. "I'll be done with my shift at ten. You call me if you need a ride anywhere else today."

"That's exactly why I didn't want you to give me a ride here in the first place. You must be exhausted."

Although he scrubbed his palm over his end-of-shift stubble, Duff shook his head. "A cup of coffee and I'm good for another three or four hours. Dad said we needed to keep an eye on you. It was an easy way to help out."

"I can take care of myself. Or, I would have been able to, except now I'm without a vehicle."

"Your partner can drive you. Or call one of the bros. You know we're here for you, baby sister." He leaned down to kiss her cheek and started backing toward the doors.

"You do realize I'm twenty-nine years old. I'm not a *baby* anything, anymore."

Duff came back a step and dropped his square jaw into her personal space to whisper, "Teasing aside, you get hurt again, and Keir or I are going to start shadowing this investigation with you."

"No."

"And after what Brower did to you, if this Gabe Knight makes you feel something again, and then throws it back in your face, there *will* be a conversation with the man."

Great. He was dead serious.

"I don't need babysitters. And I really don't need romantic help from any of you confirmed bachelors. I am working my job and living my life just fine without—" But he wasn't listening. He was leaving. "Duff? Thomas Watson Junior, I am talking to you."

He tapped his thumb and fingers together like a quacking duck. "Blah, blah, blah. Big brothers never give up taking care of their little sister. See you at Sunday dinner. Love ya."

"Grrr." Olivia fisted her free hand down at her side, feeling smothered by just how much her family loved her at that moment.

She crossed over to the bank of elevators and jabbed the call button, softly chanting a reminder that wasn't easing her frustration one bit. "They mean well—you love them. They mean well—you love them. They mean…"

She stepped into the elevator and a man darted in behind her. She recognized his musky cologne before she turned to meet his dark eyes. "Oh, great. Good morning, Marcus."

"Good morning to you, too. Glad I caught you. I know you had a rough day yesterday." He reached in front of her to close the doors before anyone else could join them. "How are you feeling, babe?"

"Babe? Really?" This day was off to a freaking fabulous start. "Have you been lying in wait for me to show up this morning?"

"I wanted to see for myself that you were all right. You got trapped in a fire. You wouldn't talk to me last night. Can't a guy worry about you?"

"Thanks for asking. I'm fine." She punched the number three. With the unsettling and aggravating things Duff had said still stewing inside her, she'd pay good money to take this ride to the third floor in silence.

But that wasn't going to happen.

"You know I'd have gotten you out of there in one piece."

Somebody else did. Blue eyes, black hair and the most masculine hands on the planet had proved utterly reliable. "I *am* in one piece."

"Are you really?"

Marcus brushed his fingers around the shell of her ear and she lurched away from the touch she wanted about as much as that answering throb of pain in her side. "Do we have to do this again?" She tried to explain her revulsion in a way that could penetrate his thick skull. "We were partners. We're not, anymore. We were going to get married. We're not, anymore. You've got no claim on my life other than being a coworker I pass in the hallway."

But there was no getting through that ego she'd once mistaken as confidence. "Come on. Just because I screwed up doesn't mean I don't still have feelings for you. I want to take care of you. Especially when you're hurt like this." He opened his arms in a humble gesture. Did he really want a hug? "You said we could still be friends."

"No. That was your idea." She pointed at him, warning him to keep his distance. "I don't need you to take care of me."

"I saw Duff drop you off."

"Family's different." Annoying and overbearing, at times, but at least she could trust them.

"You're never going to forgive me, are you?"

"I've forgiven you, Marcus." Is that what he wanted? Absolution for breaking her heart?

She herself was the one she was having such a hard time forgiving. How could she have been so sad and stupid to think she could make a relationship with her partner—a man she knew to be a player, no less—work? She'd fallen for the charm and excitement he brought to her life, for the security he'd made her feel. But that had all been a sham.

She looked up into his dark brown eyes, willing him to understand. "Forgiveness is one thing. But I'm too smart to ever forget. I don't have the feelings we once shared. I'm not that naive about relationships anymore. I've moved on. You should, too."

"I can only apologize so many times, babe. We were so good together. We have to find a way to make this work."

They passed the second floor and Olivia turned on the man she'd once loved, determined to finish this conversation before they reached their destination. "The first thing you can do is stop calling me babe. You're damn lucky I don't file a sexual harassment suit. It's Detective or Olivia or even *Hey, you*. But it will never be *babe* again."

He had the gall to laugh, although the cutting undertones revealed a taunt, not amusement. "When did you get to be such an uptight virgin again? I know who you are. I know how you like it."

"What?" She sputtered on her anger. "You son of a bitch."

There was no charm in his voice now. "I've poured out my heart to you. I've groveled as much as a man can. I tell you, I'm not the same guy I used to be." When he stepped toward her, Olivia backed against the elevator's cold steel wall, not believing this wounded anger any more than she'd believed his altruistic concern. He slapped his hand on the wall beside her and she flinched. "I want to take care of you. I'm doing everything I can to win you back. And all you've got is that you want to sue me for harassment? It'll never fly with a review board, Liv. We were engaged."

"You're threatening *me*?" Olivia shoved him out of her space as the elevator slowed its ascent. *I'm doing everything I can to win you back.* The glimmer of an idea slipped in between two angry, defensive breaths. Just how did Marcus think he was going to win her back? "You want to take care of me?"

"Yeah. Like old times."

Could he have been following her? Hoping to rescue her from an emergency like yesterday's fire so that she'd be grateful enough to take him back? Un-uh. She couldn't handle games and lies like that again. "What kind of car do you drive?"

"You want to find out? It's got a backseat where we can relieve some of that tension."

She cursed his lack of an answer as much as the innuendo. "You seriously want to go on report, don't you?" She waved aside whatever smart remark he had in mind. "Forget it." She could run Marcus's plate numbers without prolonging this conversation. She jabbed the open door button. The air in the elevator had suddenly grown toxic. "Just stay away from me."

Olivia was on her way out before the doors fully opened. But Gabe Knight was standing right there in the waiting area. Jeans. Corduroy blazer. Taut features and black hair. The full package of cynicism and strength and blue eyes that never missed a detail.

She paused for a moment to meet the silent question in those eyes. But she had too many discomfiting emotions, too many unanswered questions of her own running through her head to be in a good place to deal with him right now. When Marcus bumped her on his way out of the elevator, she took off, too, wildly hoping that Gabe was getting on that elevator and leaving.

But she knew better.

Gabe followed her through the cubicle maze to her desk. "I came to see you," his deep, low voice announced. With that and a cheery good morning from Jim at his desk, Olivia changed course and headed for the long hallway and interview rooms on the far side of the third floor. "Chief Taylor said I could sit in on meetings and interviews related to Dani's case. Maybe share some insight on what your team has come up with. I promise I won't publish any details on the case until—"

She interrupted his explanation with a pleading hand. "I'm sorry, I'm glad you've got strings to pull, but I can't do this right now." She opened the first empty room and stepped inside.

But her efforts to shut out the rest of the world for a little while were thwarted by a big foot, a strong arm and the rest of Gabe Knight coming in after her. The businesslike timbre of his voice changed as he quietly closed the door behind him. "You okay?"

Great. Now she was cornered. Olivia whirled around. "I wish everyone would stop asking me that."

"Everyone?" He stepped toward her, his demeanor infuriatingly calm. "What's wrong?"

Olivia was either ready to blow, or to burst into tears, and she wasn't about to do either one in front of an audience. She hugged her right arm over her sling and faced the corner of the room, willing her Irish blood to simmer down. "Leave me alone."

That clean, starchy scent filled her nose when he closed the distance between them. "Is this about the case? Something that guy on the elevator said? I saw him try to talk to you last night. What's got you so upset?"

The firm grasp at her elbow felt like caring concern and burst the dam of emotions she'd struggled to hold in check.

"Upset?" Olivia turned on Gabe, nudging him back toward the door. "What makes you think I'm upset? What business is it of yours, anyway?" She meant to shove him right out the door. But her hand lingered on his chest, her fingers digging into pressed cotton and warm skin. "Someone tried to kill me yesterday. Tried to kill me and a civilian who shouldn't even be involved in a police investigation. I'm trying to solve a case that a mob boss or some other sociopath doesn't want me to. I lost potential evidence. I ruined my favorite jacket. My family wants to lock me up in an ivory tower and my stupid ex thinks he can…that I want him to…"

The grip of her fingertips pulsed against Gabe's chest, absorbing heat and muscle and the bold rhythm of his heart. Olivia snatched her hand away. Why was she telling him all that? *Way to go, Watson.* Add falling for a man she shouldn't even like to the list of conflicts she had to deal with before reporting for roll call this morning.

She splayed her fingers in the air. "Can't a woman have five minutes of peace and quiet for herself?"

"Is that what you need?"

"Yes!"

With a curt nod, Gabe reached behind him and opened the door. When he closed it behind him, Olivia curled her hand around the knob, ready to shut it in his face when he tried to come back in. She held her breath, gasped, pressed her lips together, then pressed them tighter when she felt the salty grit of tears stinging her sinuses. No way was she going to give him the blackmailable advantage of seeing her bawl like an out-of-control little girl when he came back in.

Only, he didn't.

The door stayed closed. The room stayed silent.

Olivia pulled her fingers from the knob, not quite trusting the reprieve. She glanced up at the camera in the corner, glad to see the power light wasn't glowing. Although without a suspect in interrogation, there was no reason for it to be on. Was she really alone? When the silence continued, she dropped her guard and gave in to one sniffling sob.

Not exactly a bawling schoolgirl. Still, she didn't feel quite right—not her usual self, by any means.

Raking her fingers through her hair, Olivia sank into a chair and tried to pinpoint exactly what had set her off. Or maybe it'd be easier to figure out what hadn't.

She hated that Marcus could get under her skin like that. Although, she had to admit there was more suspicion and indignation than any kind of hurt when she thought of her ex. What if he was the driver who'd been following her for several days now? What was his game?

Why torment her? Did he really think she had any interest whatsoever in taking him back? Even if she did still feel something for him, she was too smart to fall for his lines again. It would only be a matter of time before he lied or cheated and hurt her again.

And what was she going to do about her brothers and dad? She didn't want to worry them. But good grief, she was on the brink of thirty and they still thought they had to watch her every move and soothe every bruise or insult or…

A shuffle of footsteps and murmur of conversation got louder outside the door. Olivia swiped the wetness off her cheeks and turned her head, bracing for the intrusion.

"The room's occupied right now." That was Gabe warning someone away from the door. "Detective Watson is working on… She's working."

"Not a problem." The voices moved on. "Atticus, let's put him in room six."

Something shifted inside her at the protective gesture. It wasn't as physical as Duff clearing a path for her through the lobby. And it wasn't the fact that a man was standing guard outside that door. Gabriel Knight had listened to what she'd asked for—to what she'd practically screamed at him—and taken her at her word.

Olivia inhaled a deep breath, and felt the tension inside her relax. She wondered for a split second if there was an ulterior motive to Gabe giving her the time she needed to regroup. But she decided it didn't matter. He'd listened to her and respected her request. When was the last time her father or grandfather or big brothers or Marcus had done that without her having to put up any kind of fight? Or give some kind of reason or reassurance?

He'd simply given her what she needed.

She took another easy breath, and another, feeling more and more like the Olivia Watson she wanted to be with every passing second.

When Gabe knocked on the door—at five minutes on the dot—and asked, "Is it safe to come in?" Olivia was on her feet.

She opened the door, wrapped her hand around the lanyard that held his visitor's ID and press pass and pulled him inside. Once the door was closed, she gave another tug, pulling his head down to hers as she stretched up to kiss the corner of his mouth. His skin was smooth this time of the morning, his sculpted lips warm and firm beneath hers. "Thank you."

His lips chased hers as she sank back onto her heels and pulled away. Gabe's blue eyes darkened and an answering fire kindled low in her belly. Yeah. She wanted this, too. Olivia slid her fingers around his neck, sliding them into the silky thickness of his hair, pulling herself back to his mouth to resume the kiss.

Only this was no grateful peck. Gabe's mouth moved over hers, the softness of her lips giving way to the demanding pressure of his. A flick of the tongue and her lips parted, welcoming his heat and passion into her eager mouth. His hands skimmed beneath her jacket, finding the nip of her waist between her gun and the sling that cradled her arm. She felt the imprint of each hand on her skin through the blouse she wore. The heat of each palm, each grasping fingertip was a vivid reminder that she was a woman beneath the trappings of first aid and her job. Goose bumps prickled across her skin at the liquid heat he was stirring inside her and she pushed up onto her toes, taking more from the kiss.

And while she suckled his lower lip between hers, Gabe widened his stance and pulled her hips into his. But the resulting friction of denim rubbing against denim wasn't enough for either of them. With a garbled moan that was as deep-pitched as his sexy voice, he walked forward until the crease beneath her bottom was wedged against the table. She felt the imprint of his belt buckle at her stomach, and the thick desire of his own response pressing into the cradle of her thighs. The molten desire unleashed by his hands molding her against his harder body seemed to gather and build a ticklish sort of pressure in her most feminine parts.

And the kiss went on.

Gabe tugged the hem of her blouse from her belt and slid one hand beneath the material to splay like a fiery brand against the small of her back and pull her impossibly closer. The other hand came up to caress the fringe of hair at her nape. He angled her head back and skidded his lips along the line of her jaw. He nibbled at her earlobe around the sterling silver stud she wore there, then closed his mouth, hot and wet over the pulse beat throbbing in her neck. Olivia gasped at the sudden spark of heat that arced through her and blurred her mind to everything but what she was feeling with this man at this moment. She was floating. On fire. Powerful. Feeling right within her own skin again.

Olivia traced her fingertips over the angles of Gabe's cheeks and jaw, the strong column of his neck, beneath the crisp starch of his collar. He held her as close as the arm folded between them allowed, and for her it wasn't enough. Her nipples puckered and pushed against the lace of her bra and she wished his capable hands were there to soothe their needy distress.

But the moment the idea of Gabe Knight stripping off her clothes and joining her on top of this table popped into her hazy thoughts, she knew she had to end the embrace.

"Gabe." She offered him one last breathless kiss, then pushed her fingers between their lips. "Gabe, we have to stop."

"I know." With a throaty growl, he pulled away, dropping little kisses to her fingertips as he retreated. Their bodies were slower to disconnect. He pulled her away from the table, peeled his hips and thighs away from hers, removed his hands from beneath her blouse and hair. He stroked his finger over her swollen, kiss-stung lips before breaking contact entirely and leaning back against the wall across from her. "I know you're right. I don't like it. But you're right."

While she adjusted her jacket and relished the air between them cooling her skin and calming the disappointed nerve endings that were still firing with the need for some kind of release, Gabe propped his hands at his waist and took several deep breaths, in through his nose, out through his mouth.

Despite the rumpled coal-dark hair and the collar she'd wrinkled with her eager hand, his deep blue eyes were as clear and focused as ever. "So why did you kiss me? And yes, I know, it was a team effort. But I'm interested in your motives."

Motives? She hadn't thought that far ahead. Still trying to regulate her own breathing, Olivia ran her fingers through her own hair, dismissing the probing question. "Don't analyze it, okay? Just accept the thank-you."

"That was more than a thank-you."

And this was more of a conversation than she wanted to have at the moment. The instinct telling her she'd be safe with Gabe had to compete with her gun-shy reticence to get involved with another man—no matter how badly her hormones or emotions might want to. Maybe if she couldn't explain what she was feeling, she could at least explain why she didn't want to discuss it.

"I've wigged out on you twice now. I usually have a better grip on things than that." Straightening her clothes with only one hand and pulled muscles proved to be a more challenging task than she'd expected. She got the sleeves and collar right, but tucking in the tail of her blouse was giving her fits, and every time she thought she had it, the sling would catch the oxford cotton and pull it loose again. "I guess I'm a little tired, a little beat-up, a little frustrated by this case. I'm sorry I let things get out of hand."

"You're not scaring me off, Detective, if that's what you're apologizing for."

"I'm not apologizing. I'm just…cautious."

Her breath caught in a soft gasp when Gabe stepped forward and batted her fingers aside to take the oxford cloth, tug it straight and tuck it securely into the waistband of her jeans for her. His assistance was quick and methodical. And though his fingers brushed against her and she embarrassed herself with a quick intake of breath, he didn't linger. "I think I'm starting to figure you out, Detective Watson. Don't fix the problem for you—give you time to think it through so you can fix it yourself. Accept that you've got this emotional armor for a reason—and that you feel safer when it's in place." He was no longer touching her, but he hadn't moved away, either, forcing her to tip her chin to meet the fathomless depths of his deep blue eyes. "Believe me, that's something I understand. This connection between us—it's completely unexpected. And, frankly, a little unsettling."

"Thanks?" But the joke fell flat because she was feeling the same way, too.

"Somewhere in my brain I guess I thought there wasn't going to be anyone after Dani." He threaded his fingers through her bangs and brushed them off her forehead. "And then you walked into my crime scene."

"Technically, that was *my* crime scene. You're the consultant and I'm the cop, remember?" She curled her fingers into her palm, fighting the itch to straighten *his* hair and moved away. "You can't feel about me the way you felt for your fiancée. We don't know each other that well."

"You are no authority on what I do or do not feel."

How could she be when she couldn't label her own emotions? That spontaneous make out session seemed to indicate they were quickly becoming something more than acquaintances or coworkers. But that didn't mean they were falling in love. And he must have loved Danielle Reese with his whole heart to remain so obsessed with her murder six years after the fact. How could she compete with that?

Olivia plucked at an imaginary fleck on her jacket. "I thought we weren't talking about it."

"That's your call, not mine. You know it's my job to get to the heart of a story." Giving her the space she'd silently asked for, Gabe propped his hip against the table and sat. "Can we talk about that guy on the elevator, then?"

Olivia puffed out a disgusted breath that buzzed her lips. "Marcus Brower was a bad choice I made. Although he did teach me a whole lot about self-reliance and learning who you can and can't trust."

"Sounds like there's more to that story."

"He's a conversation for another time. We need to get to work." He stood as she walked past him and followed her to the door. She paused before opening it and reached back to squeeze his hand. "But I do appreciate you listening to me before. Maybe it comes from growing up in a noisy house with a bunch of men. Games, music, sports, arguments. Every now and then, I just need it to be quiet."

He squeezed back before releasing her. "I'll remember that."

"Come on." Smiling and sure of herself again, Olivia opened the door to the noisy bustle of the squad room. "I'll walk you into the meeting. I wouldn't want anyone to take a shot at you."

"Because you need me to solve this case for you."

"Not exactly."

But it was scary to think how easily she could simply need *him*.

Chapter Nine

Gabe stood in the corner of the small interview room, watching Detective Sawyer Kincaid and Olivia ask questions of Ron Kober's wife, Elaine, and her attorney.

Well, mostly he watched Olivia. He'd sat through their staff meeting this morning, listening to reports about ballistics saying the gun they'd found at the warehouse was the right caliber to be the weapon used in Dani's murder, but that damage done to the barrel itself made it difficult to match the actual bullets. Further tests would have to be run to find anything conclusive. The KCFD's preliminary report on the fire indicated arson—no surprise there—but it was too soon to have a chemical analysis on the accelerant used, much less a lead on its source.

The DNA lab had even gotten an ID on the man who'd cut Gabe in the stairwell of Kober's building. Stephen March was a repeat offender with a long list of petty crimes, mostly drug related. March had been brought in for questioning on another murder a few years back, but was quickly dismissed as a suspect because of an airtight alibi—he was in a lockdown room at a rehab clinic. Maybe the guy had a knack for being in the wrong place at the wrong time. Max Krolikowski and Trent Dixon, his partner, would work on tracking

down Stephen March. They'd find out if March had wit-
nessed anything at the building he'd broken into earlier
in the week.

The Cold Case Squad's progress on finding Dani's
killer was painstakingly slow—a rehash of facts he
knew, with discussions on a few more details that would
have to be explored and double-checked before a suspect
could be brought in for questioning, much less arrested.
A week ago, Gabe would have been typing up his next
column about the square wheels of justice being stuck
in a tar pit, and that victims and perpetrators alike might
be dead by the time the department found their answers.

But today, watching Olivia in action, seeing the
wheels of memory and intelligence in those intriguing
eyes turning several steps ahead of the others at the
table, Gabe found himself looking at KCPD a little differently. Maybe even with a seed of hope taking root in
the cold morass of his cynical heart.

The other detectives and information tech at the meeting spoke and moved, but they were white noise and
blurs of shape and color that sometimes blocked Gabe's
view of the lady cop with the sleek curves and short, soft
hair. Even now, Detective Kincaid, a soft-spoken giant
of a man, the taciturn attorney and the weepy histrion-
ics of Ron Kober's widow were a mere background to
Gabe's study of Olivia.

Maybe if he hadn't kissed her. Maybe if he hadn't felt
the warmth of her supple skin or heard those tremulous
gasps of surprise and pleasure each time he touched her.
Maybe if she didn't have that red mark on her cheek or
that black sling over her arm which were direct results
of the investigative path he'd set her on. Maybe if she
hadn't awakened something more than these protective instincts inside him, he'd have been able to listen

to the update and review of evidence and suspects with a more objective ear.

Logically, he knew whatever Elaine Kober was saying now could put him closer to finding Dani's killer—or at least confirm that her late husband had been Dani's information source, and had gone to meet her the night she died. But there was something disturbingly illogical about his fascination with the knowledgeable authority in Olivia's tone, and the way her eyes had cooled from that vivid green of anger and passion to the pale gray-green they were now.

It was Olivia's interruption to the questions about Ron Kober's friends and business associates that finally shifted Gabe's focus back to the interview. "Mrs. Kober, has your husband had a lot of affairs?"

The older woman with the silvering blond hair clutched the wad of tissues she held against her heart. Her bottom lip trembled and her red-rimmed eyes widened with shock, as if the question had caught her off guard, which was probably the intent. "Affairs?" More tears began to fall and Elaine dabbed at her cheeks. "Ms. Watson, I am burying my husband tomorrow—the man I loved. I hardly think that's an appropriate question."

Olivia's voice remained gently articulate, although she didn't back down from the line of questioning. "Earlier, you said he'd *gone through* several secretaries and administrative assistants. Since it appears he pays his top staff quite generously, that may mean disagreements of a more personal nature terminated their employment. Perhaps they accused him of harassment and he paid them off." Olivia glanced down at the reports on the table in front of her, as though checking her facts. Gabe knew that folder held the arson investigator's preliminary report of the fire, but it was all part of her fact-finding game. As volatile as she'd been this morning, now that she'd had her *five minutes of peace and quiet,* Olivia was one cool customer, playing the role of mildly curious backup to Sawyer Kincaid and manipulating this interview like a pro. "Has anyone ever tried to blackmail him over his indiscretions?"

"Ron and I were married for nearly thirty years." Elaine tipped her chin and puffed up, sliding a suspicious glance to the reporter in the corner before the tears flowed freely again. "My husband's reputation... *my* reputation... I couldn't. If word got out, our children..." Another sob sucked up her words. "My little grandchildren..."

Fine, so Mrs. High Society there knew he wasn't a cop. Maybe the crying show and lack of useful answers had been for his benefit. Maybe she was truly worried about bad press smearing her late husband's name. But he wasn't here as a reporter this afternoon. Gabe walked up behind Olivia's chair. "Your answers aren't going to show up in my paper, Mrs. Kober. But you *do* need to answer Detective Watson."

Elaine's glare softened on a stuttering sob and she leaned over to whisper something to her attorney. When he nodded, she dabbed the tissues to her nose and answered. "No. No blackmail that I'm aware of."

Meaning, yes, Ron Kober had had numerous affairs. Maybe that provided a different motive for his death, one that Kincaid and Hendricks would certainly explore, but Gabe was still looking for that connection to funneling information about illegal activities to Dani six years earlier.

He had to ask. "How good a friend was Leland Asher to your late husband, Mrs. Kober?"

The widow in the black suit stiffened, seeming to take

offense at the question. "They were business acquaintances. Ron knew Mr. Asher through campaign fundraisers and the like. What does Leland have to do with Ron's death, anyway?"

Suddenly, *Mr. Asher* had become *Leland?* Interesting. Mention of the affairs left Elaine Kober weeping and rambling. But asking about a *business acquaintance* of her husband's made her sit up straight and drop the hand with her tissues into her lap. The grieving widow had disappeared.

Olivia picked up on the woman's subtle change in attitude, as well. "Your husband hasn't worked on a political campaign since he started his own PR firm. Did he and Leland Asher still take meetings or run into each other socially?"

The attorney rose and pulled out Elaine's chair to help her stand. "I'm sorry, but you've upset Elaine terribly. This interview is over. I'm driving her home." His reprimanding look included Gabe as well as the detectives. "You may contact me if you have any further questions or developments to share in her husband's tragic death."

After the two of them had gone, Gabe tapped Sawyer Kincaid on the shoulder. "I'd follow up on her whereabouts during the time of the murder. Hell hath no fury like a woman cheated on."

Olivia dodged her gaze from Sawyer's quick glance, making Gabe wonder what that exchange was all about. But Olivia stood, still in work mode. "I'd check the affair angle with Kober's former staff, too," she suggested. "One of them may have been looking for retribution."

"Already on it." The oversize detective pushed back his chair and stood. "Joe's got Kober's latest assistant, Misty Harbison, the woman who found his body, in Interview 3. If she and Kober were seeing each other outside of work, we'll find out and let you know. And if she can link him to Leland Asher or your dead reporter, we'll keep you posted on that, too."

Olivia smiled. "Thanks for letting us sit in, Sawyer."

"Not a problem." He traded nods with Gabe before leaving. "Mr. Knight."

"Kincaid." Gabe knew better than to expect warm fuzzies from the department he'd once criticized for moving too slowly at solving cases. But he appreciated Sawyer Kincaid and the members of Olivia's team tolerating his presence. He glanced down at Olivia. "Elaine got ticked off when you asked…"

"Did you hear that slipup?" Olivia chimed in at the same time. They both grinned at the shared thought. "Somebody knows Leland Asher better than she wants us to believe. We need to find out how those two are connected. Either she's aware of Asher threatening her husband—maybe she's been threatened, too—or there's a personal connection we don't know about."

"Do we follow up on that or sit in on Miss Harbison's interview?"

"I think Sawyer and Joe have the affair angle covered." Olivia tucked the folder beneath her left arm and sling, and paused in front of the closed door.

For a split second, Gabe's pulse leaped with the anticipation of revisiting what had happened the last time they were alone in an interview room together. But he quickly put the brake on those thoughts. Olivia was thinking, moving puzzle pieces, intriguing him in an equally compelling way. "What is it?"

"I bet Miss Harbison could get us a look at Kober's appointment calendar for the past few months."

"See if he met with Leland Asher or one of his lieutenants?"

"And if she's worried about being called out on an affair, I'm guessing she'd be more cooperative than Mrs. Kober was." She pulled out her phone and texted a message. "I'll have Sawyer ask for a copy."

Gabe tapped the edge of her phone. "See if she can get us Mrs. Kober's appointment calendar, too."

"Smart man." Once the request was sent, she looked up at Gabe. "This is still speculation, of course," she reminded him.

"I know. Without Dani's flash drive we can't prove Kober was her informant. And without proving that, there's no motive for someone in Asher's or Senator McCoy's camp to kill him."

"We need to connect those two if we want any chance of proving that was the motive for Dani's murder. But until we get a clue to the location of that flash drive, this is a lead we can pursue." She pocketed her phone and opened the door. "I'll check Kober's social calendar, too. Even a casual conversation at a fund-raising event could have been an opportunity to threaten him about keeping mum regarding any links to McCoy's campaign."

"So we need guest lists."

Olivia grinned. "Paperwork is the best part of this job."

Even if the sarcasm wasn't so blatant, Gabe would have to disagree. He closed the door to the interview room and followed Olivia to her desk where she started making phone calls.

The best part of this job was watching Olivia Watson in action.

THE HOST PACED to the far side of the room and back again before taking a seat behind the large desk. "Are you nuts?"

"Don't say that to me." The young man stopped twisting his fingers together long enough to take offense. "You said that no one could ever suspect me."

"No one does."

But the gentle tone was no more soothing than the angry outburst had been. "That detective is figuring everything out. I could tell by the way she and that reporter were looking at pictures and breaking into things." He pawed at his own hands with a nervous mania again. "What if they found the gun?"

"Is it your gun?"

The young man shook his head. "You know you gave it to me."

"And you did what I told you to afterward, didn't you?"

He scraped his fingers through his dull hair and nodded. "I stuck a screwdriver into the barrel and scratched it all up. I wore gloves and I wiped it clean, just like you said." But he grabbed the desktop and pulled himself to the edge of his chair. "She's showed up where I am two times in two days. That's trouble for me, I can tell."

If this scheme unraveled because this stupid little tweaker couldn't curb his paranoia, then a more drastic means of ensuring his silence would have to be used. "I have professional friends who get paid a lot of money to take care of loose ends like Detective Watson and Gabriel Knight. I will deal with them." The host leaned forward, sheer proximity making the young man slink back into his chair. "Don't make me think you're becoming a loose end. Or I'll have to deal with you, too."

The young man was literally shaking with fear, or maybe crashing off his meth. "But you promised you'd help me."

"I have helped you, time and time again. All I've ever asked in exchange is that you listen to me, trust me."

He seemed to consider the advice, but ultimately rejected it and started pleading again. "I have to protect my family. That's the only reason I killed for you. You know that. If something happens to me—"

"Were my instructions completely clear?" The host stood, seizing the opportunity to drive the threat home.

"Yes."

"And you followed them to the letter?"

The cowering young man nodded.

"Thanks to me, you've gotten away with murder. Don't give in to these panic attacks. Leave the detective and her friend to me."

"But—"

"Go home. Keep your mouth shut. Do exactly as I say…or there won't be anyone around who can keep your family safe."

Chapter Ten

He'd served his time.

When the hands on his watch flipped to nine o'clock, Gabe swallowed the last of the tepid champagne he'd been nursing all evening, and set the flute on the next waiter's tray that went past. While he was happy to do this favor for Mara Boyd, and attend the elegant soiree along with hundreds of wealthy donors, state and local politicians and a cadre of reporters, he was more than ready to be done. He unhooked the button behind his bow tie and pulled out his cell phone, heading past mammoth oil paintings to the wide marble stairs that would take him out the Nelson-Atkins Museum of Art's original entrance into the covered walkway that led to the parking garage.

He was looking for a text or voice mail from Olivia, hoping she'd share whatever she found after he'd left her at the precinct office to get ready for tonight's black-tie gala. He wished he was with her instead of marking time at this see-and-be-seen social event, even if she was still glued to her desk and phone and endless mug of coffee. Working side by side with Olivia these past few days, Gabe had discovered a sense of drive and intellect that was his equal, if not his better, and he found that invigorating and as irresistible as the velvety waves of her hair.

He paused halfway down the steps and frowned at the blank screen on his phone.

Nothing. No word on whether they were getting the Kobers' appointment schedules or not, or if Misty Harbison had admitted to an affair. Nothing. He wondered if that meant she hadn't found anything or if she just didn't want to share the information with him. Then, not liking the instant internal debate as to which explanation bothered him more, Gabe tucked his phone into the chest pocket of his black tuxedo jacket and continued down to the ground floor.

Maybe she'd simply gotten tired and had gone out for a decent cup of coffee. Or the ache in her pulled muscles had gotten bad enough that she'd taken a pain pill and gone to bed. But if she had found something, and thought she was leaving him out of the loop on any part of this investigation, then she didn't know him at all. He'd call her as soon as he got to the privacy of his car and demand an update.

He'd made nice with the mayor and gotten a couple of good sound bites from her for his column tomorrow. He'd let his boss decide whether the standard promises to repair streets, grow the economy and bring more green space to KC's urban environment were compelling enough to earn the *Journal*'s endorsement. He'd chatted with his colleagues and listened to Adrian McCoy's support the party speech. He was beginning to understand Olivia's aversion to an endless barrage of conversations and noise because right now, all he wanted was to be alone in the quiet confines of his car and get a hold of her.

Quickening his steps through the clusters of guests sharing conversations and admiring displays, Gabe headed through the museum's open bronze doors and turned down the ramp leading to the parking garage. But a bottleneck of people entering and leaving the museum gift shop near the exit stopped him. Craning his neck, he searched for the best path and excused his way through the crowd. But just when the bank of glass exit doors was in reach, Gabe halted.

The crowd filled in around him as his gaze landed on the stout man with dramatic silver sideburns and a pretty brunette on his arm—Leland Asher.

It had been some time since Gabe had met face-to-face with the alleged crime boss. His companion was different, a more mature woman than the bimbo he'd seen him with six years ago when Gabe had pressed the man for answers. The bodyguard lurking behind his shoulder was the same loyal hulk who'd prevented Gabe from getting too close to his boss at any time since. A young man Gabe didn't recognize completed the entourage. He was too short and skinny to offer much protection, so Gabe was guessing a nephew, or even an accountant or attorney on Asher's payroll.

But knowing that only a couple of people in the loitering crowd stood between him and the man whose illegal activities had inspired Dani's last story, and almost certainly sealed her fate, wasn't the most startling observation.

It was the fact that Adrian McCoy, the state senator Ron Kober had once worked for, the politician who'd taken money from Asher, according to the notes he'd read the night Dani had been murdered, was standing close enough to Leland Asher to shake hands. Had the two men been thrown together by the jostling of the other guests? Or was this "accidental" meeting no accident at all?

Whatever the two men were discussing, the din of

the crowd made it impossible to hear. Leland smiled. The senator nodded. Leland patted the senator on the shoulder and Adrian McCoy smiled.

Then one of Senator McCoy's handlers spotted Gabe zeroing in on them, and the entourage of aides and security quickly escorted the senator out the door.

Leland and his crew exited into the garage, too. But Gabe pushed through the remaining crowd and hurried out the door after them, catching the group at the valet stand. "Mr. Asher." He pointed to the car with the state flags pulling away toward the garage exit. "Care to comment on what just happened between you and Senator McCoy?"

The bodyguard put his hand on Gabe's chest and pushed him back a step, but Leland ordered his man to stand aside. "It's all right, Dominic. I'm not afraid of the press." The self-important lout smiled. "The senator and I exchanged pleasantries. I wished him well on his reelection campaign."

"Any idea why the senator and his team hustled him away from you as quickly as they could? Perhaps they want to distance their candidate from a man who's been investigated for making illegal campaign contributions in exchange for government contracts, tax breaks and other considerations."

"You're like a dog with a bone, aren't you, Knight?" His smile widened, but never reached his eyes. "As I recall, our fine police department cleared me of any charges of collusion. A fact which your paper printed."

"There's a difference between clearing your name and not having enough evidence yet to make a charge stick." Gabe kept the bodyguard in his line of sight and moved in closer. "I stand by my article— I never said you were innocent, only that KCPD wasn't able to make a case against you."

"Well, they've absolutely cleared my name of the murder of your fiancée that you keep trying to pin on me. As you well know, I was at my niece's wedding in Saint Louis on the night poor Miss Reese died."

"Leland…" The dark-haired woman rested her hand on her escort's arm, quietly diverting his attention. "Let's not ruin the evening by reopening old wounds."

"It's all right, Bev. This is business." He patted her hand with his thick fingers and directed her to the limousine that was pulling up. "You run along. I'll be quick. I promise." Leland leaned in to kiss Bev's cheek and handed her off to the young man.

But Gabe noted the older man wasn't willing to stand here and face him alone. He nodded for Dominic to wait right behind his shoulder.

"What game are you playing now, Asher?"

"No games, I assure you, Mr. Knight. If you have questions, ask them. I don't want you printing that I didn't cooperate with the press."

Gabe refused to back down from the subtle show of intimidation. "I saw you talking to Senator McCoy. Did Ron Kober's name come up? That's convenient for both of you to have him out of the picture."

"I may have extended condolences. But Mr. Kober was loyal to his former employer. He would never betray him by telling lies to some upstart reporter."

"You mean feeding information to Danielle Reese."

"That's where this interview is headed, isn't it? Don't they all come back to your accusations that I was somehow involved in your fiancée's death?" That big fake smile vanished. "I know you and your girlfriend are looking into my affairs. The lovely detective *is* your girlfriend, isn't she?"

Gabe bristled. The girlfriend part felt right, yet didn't feel big enough to describe the feelings for Olivia growing inside him. Still, that carefully worded statement got under his skin and put him more on guard than the hulking shadow behind Leland Asher did. "What do you know about Detective Watson?"

"I know she's Thomas Watson's daughter."

"You know her father?"

"We've had conversations over the years. Some less pleasant than others. He seems to think I know things."

"I'm sure your ignorance frustrated him."

"From what I hear, Ms. Watson is a bulldog like he was." Asher gave a mock fist pump. "Truth, justice and the Kansas City way. Determined to live on her own, determined to forge her own successful career, even after that embarrassing setback with her partner, Marcus Brower."

Right. The jerk on the elevator who'd set Olivia off this morning. Other than calling Brower her ex, Olivia had been closemouthed about her former partner. But with the look Sawyer Kincaid had given her when they'd discussed Ron Kober cheating on his wife, and the hints Leland Asher was dropping now, Gabe was beginning to piece together a relationship that had been more personal than professional. A relationship that had ended badly. The fact Asher seemed to know more about Olivia's past than he did stuck in his craw…yet reignited that protective urge that seemed to flare up whenever his thoughts turned to her. A reputed crime boss had no business knowing that much about a cop.

"Detective Watson is one of Kansas City's Finest," Gabe insisted. "If she's on your trail, you'd better be looking over your shoulder. No matter how long it takes, she and her team will solve Dani's murder."

"I don't know about that. I saw a picture of the two of you in the paper, with that story about last night's fire." The portly man clicked his tongue against his teeth in a pitying *tsk-tsk*. "You seem to be an exceptionally bad-luck charm for the women you get involved with. She might survive longer without you."

Gabe ignored the stab of guilt Asher had intended to inflict. "Is that a threat?"

"I wouldn't threaten a police officer." Asher touched the handkerchief in his chest pocket and sighed as if truly offended. "I don't know what kind of man you think I am, Mr. Knight."

"Off the record?" Gabe leaned in to whisper in his ear. "I think you're a greedy SOB who's taken advantage of this town and gotten away with murder, or, at least, murder for hire."

Asher was smiling again when Gabe backed away. "It's a good thing your opinion doesn't matter. I certainly won't be going to jail for a crime I did not commit. You and Ms. Watson be careful about pursuing this, or I'll be taking you both to court for harassment and defamation of character."

Gabe shook his head at the man's venom-laced charm. "You're responsible for Dani. And I'm guessing you're responsible for Ron Kober's murder, too."

"And I'm guessing that, after all this time, you still can't prove a damn thing. Neither will your cop girlfriend."

"I'll take that bet."

"I'm a tough businessman, Mr. Knight. I've made millions and I've made enemies. I don't apologize for that.

But I'm not this serial killer you seem to think I am. I never even met Miss Reese, and Ron Kober was a friend."

A line from Elaine Kober's curtailed interview this afternoon replayed in Gabe's head. "His wife seems to think you were just a business acquaintance."

Asher shrugged. "That's how we met, of course. But I've known Ron and Elaine for several years. I should call on her—I imagine she's struggling right now and could use the support. I hope you're not pestering her with these incessant questions."

"Then maybe you should start answering a few, so she doesn't have to."

"Blame me if you want for whatever difficulties Elaine is going through right now. Because, even though you've yet to prove anything, in your book, apparently, I'm guilty of every wrongdoing in this city." He twisted the signet ring on his left pinkie finger, then casually adjusted his cuffs and cufflinks. "Just think, if something was to happen to your detective friend right now, you'd probably accuse me of hurting her, too. But look…" He opened his arms, gesturing to the guests inside by the gift shop and filtering through the glass doors to the parking garage. "I have hundreds of people who can verify where I am, and that I had nothing to do with it…including you."

A chill ran down Gabe's spine. "Nothing to do with what?"

"Just giving an example of how wrong you are about me. This interview is over, Mr. Knight. Dominic?" Leland's bodyguard led the way to the limo and opened the back door for his boss. When Gabe caught a peek inside the tinted windows of the long black car, he saw the young man on his cell phone, staring right back at

Gabe as he relayed some kind of message to the caller at the other end of the line.

What the hell? Gabe read the threat between the lines—Asher's calm demeanor, the cryptic words, maybe even the twist of his ring—it all meant something. He didn't bother chasing Asher to his limo and demanding straight answers. For once, he didn't try to make sense of all the details. There was just one glaring fact that mattered. He and Olivia must be getting close to uncovering the truth.

So what were Asher and his cronies willing to do to stop them?

Gabe slapped the departing limousine out of his way and ran down the parking aisle to his SUV. He pulled out his phone and punched in Olivia's number before unlocking the door and getting inside to start the engine.

The number rang and rang. "What kind of cop doesn't answer her phone?" Gabe's stomach knotted as tightly as it had when he'd seen her plunge beneath that twisted stair railing toward the fire beneath them. But he couldn't just reach out and save her this time. "Come on, Liv. Pick up."

He glanced behind him, seeing the vehicles of departing guests starting to line up. He shifted the Chevy into Reverse and backed out of the parking stall, then sped as quickly as he dared toward the nearest exit before he got blocked behind traffic.

When the call finally went to voice mail, his warning was brief. "It's Gabe. Leland Asher is up to something. Be careful, love—Liv," he corrected before disconnecting the call and dropping the phone into the console beside him. He swung out into the street, flipped on his headlights and stepped on the gas. Let one of Kansas City's Finest try to stop him now.

What difference did it make if he'd let it slip that he had feelings for Olivia? If she was in danger and he couldn't reach her, what difference did anything he said or did make at all?

OLIVIA PUT HER PHONE on speaker mode and set it on top of the papers spread across her desk. Picking up Chinese takeout and changing into yoga pants, tennis shoes and an old flannel shirt she'd inherited from Duff were the only concessions she'd made to going off duty and relaxing at home. But the work hadn't stopped. Since she was taking a break from poring over Ron Kober's schedule for the past several months, she stood up beside the oak desk and did some of the stretches her physical therapist had recommended to speed the healing of the sprained muscles in her shoulder and side. "Hey, Niall. What's up?"

"Hey, Livvy." The least chatty of all her family, Olivia's middle brother skipped any small talk and got straight to his reason for calling. "I finished my autopsy on Ron Kober. I've sent a copy of the report to Detectives Kincaid and Hendricks, but I know you were curious about a couple of things, too."

Olivia smiled when she heard that he'd remembered her request. "Cause of death?"

"Blunt force trauma to the head. Blood and brain matter on the trophy the CSIs brought in confirm it as the murder weapon." Her smile became a grimace of *eeuw* at the details her brother discussed so casually. "I'm not the one who pieces together the clues, but it couldn't look any less like a professional hit."

Feeling a combination of gross-out and disappointment, Olivia gave up on the multitasking and sank onto the leather desk chair. She hugged her knees to her chest.

"So you believe his death was a crime of passion, not anything planned or carried out professionally?"

"Like I said—I just look at what the body tells me. He had bruising on his knuckles, too, so there may have been some sort of struggle." What struggle? Kober's office had been as neat as a magazine picture, other than the body, the murder weapon and the bloodstains beneath him. "The killer probably grabbed the trophy as a weapon of opportunity to defend herself."

"Well, somebody had time to clean up. What do you estimate as the time of death?"

"Somewhere between nine and eleven that morning."

Olivia shuffled through the papers on top of her desk to find Sawyer's initial report. Kober's secretary, Misty Harbison, had called 9-1-1 shortly after one that afternoon saying she'd discovered his body. The police had arrived by one-fifteen. Three or four hours was plenty of time to set the private office to rights. But why hadn't anyone seen or heard an argument? And why would Leland Asher, or anyone he might hire, create such a messy crime scene, and then have to spend time there cleaning it up? The risk of being discovered was too great.

"Wait a minute." Olivia dropped her feet to the floor and leaned closer to the phone. "You said *herself?*"

Niall chuckled. "I wondered if you picked up on that. Don't worry. I've already passed on the UNSUB details to Detective Kincaid. Mr. Kober was struck three times. The first blow might have made him dizzy, but wouldn't have rendered him unconscious. He was still fighting. The second blow took him down, and the third finished him off. Whoever was swinging that trophy didn't have the upper body strength to deal a single killing blow. Plus, the angle of the first two wounds indicates Kober's assailant was slightly shorter than he was."

Olivia thought of the young man in the gray hoodie who'd been so desperate to sneak out of that building and avoid the cops. What was his name? She flipped to another page in another report. Stephen March. "Niall, could his killer have been a short, slightly built man?"

"It's possible. But even wiry guys, unless they have some kind of handicap, would be stronger than these blows indicate."

She thought of the knife wound on Gabe's forearm. Although the wound had been deep enough to require stitches, the ER doctor had said it could have been much worse. Olivia had dismissed Stephen March as a hesitant attacker, a man more interested in getting away than in inflicting harm. But could March have some kind of physical impairment that weakened his strength? She flipped to a clean sheet of her notepad and jotted a reminder to do a medical background check before Max and Trent brought March in for his interview tomorrow.

"You still there, Livvy?" Niall asked. "Or are you putting a puzzle together?"

"You know me." Although she suspected Niall's autopsy report would be of more use to Kincaid and Hendricks in solving Ron Kober's murder, she wasn't giving up on the idea that this crime would lead her to answers on Danielle Reese's murder. Gabe was so certain the two deaths were related that somewhere along the way he'd convinced her, too. "What about the other thing I asked you to check?"

"You were right. I did find a small wad of torn-up gray paper in the victim's stomach." She heard a few clicks on a keyboard and suspected Niall was calling up the information on his computer. "I didn't find signs of trauma to the mouth or throat, so I'm guessing he ate it voluntarily."

Probably an impromptu effort to hide the note from his attacker. "I don't need any gross details about the acidic properties of stomach contents, but was there any message on the note?"

"The only thing I could make out on the paper was a name. 'E. Zeiss.'" She copied down the name Niall spelled for her. "They were on two separate strips of paper, with one fitting above the other, so there may have been more to the *E* and the rest of the message, but that's all I could recover." Niall's sigh was either a yawn or a stretch, an indicator that his workday had been as long as hers. "Is that enough information to keep you busy for the rest of the night?"

He knew her far too well. "Thanks, Dr. Watson," she teased.

"Not a problem, Sherlock. Are you feeling better today?"

"I am after talking to my favorite brother."

Niall laughed. "You say that to all of us, don't you."

She laughed along with him. "Maybe."

"Love ya, kiddo."

"Love you."

Olivia hung up to find she had a missed call and message from Gabe. And though the idea of hearing that deep, sexy voice stirred a warm flutter of anticipation inside that no longer made her feel as defensive as it did even a few days ago, she wanted to finish compiling the circumstantial and forensic evidence she'd gathered. She wanted to be prepared with answers to the follow-up questions she was certain he'd ask when she called back to share these new developments on the investigation.

She went back to the photocopies of Ron Kober's appointments the morning of his death. It looked as though two appointments and a staff meeting had been canceled.

Plus, he'd given Misty, his assistant, the morning off. The man had cleared his schedule, cleared his entire office that morning except for the appointment penciled in at nine o'clock.

"Zeiss." Olivia read the word out loud, then turned on another lamp over her desk and pulled the phone book from the top drawer. "Z, Z, Zeiss. Hmm."

There were only two Zeisses in the Kansas City directory, but neither one had a first name that started with an *E*. Avoiding a random search through the yellow pages, Olivia picked up her phone to run an online search.

"Zeiss Security." Now that was interesting. Based in the KC area, the Zeiss Security website offered private security and investigation services. "An empty private office with no chance of being interrupted." And Kober's building already had a team of security guards.

Ron Kober had hired a private investigator. But who or what was he investigating? Whatever he'd learned at that meeting might have been the thing that had gotten him killed. Whoever met with Kober should at least be questioned as a potential suspect or witness. She wrote down the company's phone number and made a mental note to call them as soon as they were open for business in the morning. Since their client was dead, they might ignore any confidentiality agreement and share their information without having to get a subpoena.

With a buzz of renewed excitement humming through her veins at the forward progress she was making on the case, Olivia called her voice mail and put Gabe's message on speaker phone while she straightened all the paperwork on her desk. Way to kill the buzz.

"Leland Asher?" Had Gabe had a run-in with the reputed crime boss?

"Be careful, love—Liv."

"*You* be careful," she warned the inanimate phone. But was it Gabe's urgent tone or the slip of the tongue endearment that made her emotions snap?

Olivia scooped up her phone to call Gabe back and remind him he had neither the authority, the proof nor the secure backup to accuse Leland Asher of anything. What was that stubborn, determined man thinking? By reopening the investigation, they were bound to stir up old secrets and make a murderer who'd been living free for six years decidedly uncomfortable and therefore unpredictable. If Asher was up to something, shouldn't the man who'd been accusing him of murder for six years be the one who should be worried about some kind of retribution?

Olivia pulled up Gabe's number, grateful for his concern, yet frightened that he didn't seem to practice the same caution about his own safety. "If you don't answer this phone, Gabe Knight, I'm going to—"

A thump against her front window stopped the complaint and the call. Olivia turned toward the picture window behind her couch, catching her breath and going on alert when she saw a blur of a shadow dancing across the sheer curtains there. She might have dismissed it as the streetlamp across the street shining through the branches of the sugar maple in her front yard. A breeze could have stirred the branches and startled her.

But the lamp and the tree were permanent fixtures, and that shadow had disappeared.

The hackles at the back of her neck shivered with a clear warning.

Someone had moved past her window.

With the lamps on over her desk, the peeping Tom would have been able to see her in here working. He'd have at least been able to see her silhouette in front of the desk and track her movements. Was that the threat Gabe had been so cryptic about? Did he think Leland Asher was coming after her?

Without wasting a moment to think of all the possible motives for being spied on, Olivia leaned over the desk and killed the lights. She dropped her phone into the chest pocket of her shirt, picked up her keys and headed through the dark house to her bedroom where she opened the closet and pulled the lockbox that held her gun and ammo off the shelf.

Once the box was unlocked and she was armed, she pressed the safety off her Glock and crept through the remodeled 1950s bungalow, scanning each window for signs of curious eyes until she ended up back in the living room. When she peeked behind the edge of the curtain, there was no one outside. She knew she hadn't imagined that shadow. Maybe the pervert had startled himself when he'd hit the window and run away.

"That's right, pal," she whispered, moving toward the front door. She knew she wouldn't be able to drop her guard and rest until she saw with her own eyes that the threat had vanished or been neutralized. "You picked the wrong lady to spy on."

After unhooking the security chain and dead bolt, Olivia slipped out onto the porch. Keeping her ears alert to the sounds of running footsteps or a car speeding away, she moved down the steps and across the yard, with her gun firmly gripped between both hands. The neighborhood was quiet. Other than the two streetlamps on the block, and the glow of a few late-night lights through curtains and closed doors, there wasn't anyone stirring inside or out. So either the peeping Tom had run away or he was still here somewhere, hiding in the shadows, holding his breath.

Olivia turned her back on the shadows for a cautious moment to squat down between the shrubs and her front window. She touched her fingertips to the impressions in the soft dirt there. Definitely not her imagination.

Those were footprints, man-size and deep enough to suspect that her spy had been there a long time. Watching. Waiting to see more than her silhouette through the drapery sheers. The flower buds broken off her forsythia bushes indicated he'd tripped over them in his haste to get away once discovered.

A shiver of uncomfortable awareness raised goose bumps across her skin and Olivia turned. Someone was *still* watching. But from where?

With her eyes adjusted to the dimness of the late spring night, she didn't bother retrieving a flashlight to aid in her search. With a quick look around the landscaping, and even up into the tree, she determined the yard was clear. But she couldn't account for every yard and every house or the smattering of cars parked along the curb. Keeping her gun pointed down at the concrete, Olivia quickly moved to the end of her driveway to gain an unobstructed view of the small suburban homes up and down the street. Other than the flickering lights of television sets through closed curtains, there was no activity at all. No trees or bushes stirring except with the rhythmic sway of the breeze. There were no neighbors out for a late-night walk with their dog, no teenager sneaking home from a party, no signs of movement at all except…

A shift in the shadows farther down the street darted past the corner of her eye. Trusting her instincts more than her vision right now, Olivia turned.

The black car.

"You son of a…" The engine turned over and roared to life. The driver knew he'd been spotted.

Forget stealth now. Besides, she was in the mood to let Marcus Brower have it for freaking her out like this.

"Marcus!" she shouted, raising her gun and walking into the middle of the street so he could see her and the Glock and know she meant business. "Get out of the—"

The headlights flashed on, straight to high beams, blinding her. Squinting her eyes against the painful shock to her retinas, she averted her gaze and fired up her temper.

"Damn you." She didn't have her badge, but no one could doubt her authority as she marched down the street. She aimed her gun at the closest headlight. "KCPD! Get out of the car right now." The motor revved and Olivia cursed the driver's defiance. She arced her path toward the opposite curb, still trying to get a bead on the man behind the wheel. But the lights were too bright. "Marcus, turn off the engine and get out. Now!"

But just as the loathsome man rolled down the tinted window to give her a glimpse at his face, she heard a shout. "Leave the dead alone!"

The powerful engine roared into overdrive. The car swung away from the curb and barreled toward her. Olivia braced her feet and aimed at the lights. But she was in a residential neighborhood, firing blind, so she lowered her weapon and backed away. But the lights grew large, like angry eyes, and the car chased her down like a giant predator charging its prey, forcing her to turn and run.

Olivia dove into the neighbor's yard across the street, tumbling over the sidewalk, wrenching her bruised shoulder. She heard the bang of the car jumping the curb and felt its heat bearing down on her.

She was on her knees, trying to regain her footing and find a target when the blare of long horn joined the attack. The black car shifted course, plowing up a ravine in the grass, tossing up clods of sod and gravel that pinged against her skin.

Porch lights popped on like fireworks going off. The horn kept honking. Since her feet weren't cooperating, Olivia rolled over onto her bottom and sat up, firing off a shot at the black car as it hopped the curb back into the street and sped away. She put out one taillight before it careened around the corner.

Ignoring the twinge in her arm, she pushed to her hands and knees. She instinctively recoiled from the screech of brakes in the street beside her and the second set of lights shining on her. She managed to stand, but swayed on her feet when she tried to run.

"Olivia!" Two strong arms grabbed her, pulling her against a wall of warmth and strength, trying to steady her. "Are you hurt?"

She knew the deep voice, knew the touch. But she pushed Gabe's arms away and stumbled back into the street as the black car's taillight disappeared beyond the houses in the next block. "He got away. That son of a bitch got away. Again."

"Come on." Gabe was on his phone, reporting the incident, following right behind her. His hand pressed into the small of her back, guiding her off the street as she pulled out her own phone. "You go back in the house while I move my SUV off the street."

"Damn you, Marcus Brower." Ignoring Gabe's order, Olivia planted her feet on the walkway in front of her porch and punched in a number she remembered far too well.

"Yep?"

"Marcus. Since when did you take up stalking?"

"Liv? What are you talking about? Are you all right?"

"Barely in one piece, no thanks to you. What kind of car do you drive?"

"I don't. Why do you keep asking that? I bought a red pickup after we split, and I still have that motorcycle we used to cruise on. Mmm. Hold that thought a sec."

"Excuse me?"

And then the background sounds registered. Soft music. Giggling. Moans. Not one indication of a speeding car or traffic. "Do you need a lift somewhere? I'm kind of busy at the moment."

She'd interrupted a make-out session. Yeah, he was real heartbroken over losing her. And she wasn't. Not anymore.

Olivia disconnected the call. All she felt was confusion. Marcus wasn't driving the black car. So who was following her? Who just tried to kill her? Or tried again, she suspected, thinking back to the fire. Who was the creeper getting in her head and messing with her life?

She clutched her arm to her side and slowly turned, looking around her for answers that wouldn't come. She recognized each of her neighbors, at their doors, on their porches, inspecting the damage done to their yard. No one was hurt. No one was a threat. She recognized the tall man on his cell phone striding toward her. The tuxedo Gabe wore didn't make any more sense than the rest of this.

Then she remembered an odd phrase and whispered, "Leave the dead alone."

"What did you say?" Gabe's hand was at her back

again. Warm. Supportive. A link to the reality just beyond her reach. The black car wasn't about an old relationship gone wrong. This was about a case. This was
about Dani Reese's murder. "What's that?" Gabe was
answering the dispatcher on his phone. "That's right.
Black Challenger. The last three numbers were 487. I
know it's only a partial, but I'm certain of the make."

Olivia was cradling her left arm at her side, rubbing
her shoulder. Suddenly, the aches in her body lessened.
She tipped her face up to his taut features. "You got a
plate number?"

Gabe tucked his phone away and nodded. "I gave the
description to 9-1-1. I've already talked to your partner,
Jim. He's on his way. He'll take care of the neighbors
and securing your place."

What else had she missed? "When did you call Jim?"

"On my way over. Jim's your partner. He's supposed
to back you up, isn't he?" Olivia nodded. Yes. Trusting
Jim Parker felt right. "I didn't know if your brothers or
dad would stay on the line once they knew it was me.
After my little chat with Leland Asher at the reception
tonight, I needed someone to be with you. I didn't know
if I'd get here in time."

"Do you think that was one of Asher's men? What
kind of mob boss hires a peeping Tom?" She pointed at
the window where the perp had hidden in the bushes.
"I've been alone since dinner. He could have broken in
at any time. But he was just…looking."

"You're not making me feel any better about what just
happened… Ah, hell." Gabe pinched her chin between
his thumb and forefinger and tilted her face toward the
streetlamp. He pulled the pristine white handkerchief
from his jacket pocket and pressed it against her cheek.
She winced at the sting on her skin, but he didn't apolo-

gize. "You've opened that scrape again." When she took over holding the compress against her cheek, he dropped his gaze to her gun. "Is that thing secure?"

Olivia reset the safety. "It's safe."

He scanned over his shoulder at the neighbors. "You've got a lot of curious eyes on you right now. Should we go inside?"

She nodded, but didn't move.

"Olivia? Come on, love." That snapped her gaze up to his. He led her into the house and closed and locked the door behind him. She stood in the foyer watching him do the things she should have been doing. He flipped on the porch light and faced her again. "Do you need five minutes before police cars and an ambulance arrive?"

Alone? That was the last thing she wanted right now. Liv—love— He'd said it twice now, and she wasn't going to argue about the mix-up. "No." She set her gun down on the credenza beside the door, turned and walked into his chest. He was warm. He was solid. He was as real as a man could get. When his arms folded around her, she finally drew in a deep, calming breath. "I need you to hold me. Just hold me."

The arm behind her waist hugged her tightly against him. His other hand slid up to cup the cool skin at her nape. "Finally. I wasn't even sure you knew how worried I was about you."

Olivia slipped her hands beneath his jacket and turned her undamaged cheek into the pillow of his shoulder, burrowing into his warmth. "I hate it when I don't have the answers. When I can't settle my brain, I can't relax. I have all these pieces to the puzzle, but I can't make them fit together yet."

"Can I help?"

She tried to slow her racing thoughts to match the steady beat of his heart beneath her ear. "You are."

His fingers moved against her skin, massaging the tension there. "Tell me about the pieces that don't fit."

"Do you know an E. Zeiss?" Gabe shook his head. "Did Dani's notes indicate any reason why Ron Kober would hire a private detective?"

"No."

"I don't suppose the number thirty-six twenty means anything to you, either."

The massage at her nape stilled. "Thirty-six twenty?"

"It was on a shred of paper in Kober's office. He ate the rest of the note just before he…" Wait a second. The deep timbre of Gabe's tone had changed. Olivia leaned back against his arm and tilted her gaze to his. "You know what it means."

His nostrils flared with a resolute breath. With his arm at her back, he turned her to escort her into the hallway. "I want you to pack a bag."

If he had an answer, she needed it. Skipping a step ahead of him, she spun around and parked herself in his path. "Why? Where are we going?"

"I'm not leaving you here by yourself tonight. Even with your partner patrolling around outside, it doesn't feel safe." His blue eyes were dark like midnight, the careworn lines etched more deeply beside them. "I lost Dani because I wasn't paying attention to the details. I wasn't close enough to help save her."

That driving need to find answers abated beneath the compassionate tug on her heart. Olivia closed the distance between them, smoothing the lapels of his jacket and fiddling with the bow tie hanging loose from beneath his collar. Gabriel Knight was a confident man, as compulsive as she could be, sure of his goals and unafraid to pursue the truth. Yet there was this chink in his armor, this wounded place inside him where his love for Dani and his guilt over losing her still had a cruel grip on him.

Gabe Knight was a stunner in his tuxedo—sexy and sophisticated and maybe a little bit dangerous—but that wasn't what prompted Olivia's carefully worded invitation. "I know things have happened fast between us, and I like the idea of keeping an eye on each other. Maybe… you could stay here."

He threaded his fingers through her bangs and brushed them gently off her forehead before leaning in to kiss her. She felt the light touch of gratitude and apology before his lips moved over hers in a hard, sensuous kiss that gave her a brief taste of the desire arcing between. But before she could stretch up on tiptoe to answer that driving need, Gabe pulled away. He turned her down the hallway, swatted her rump and scooted her on her way. "Not if you want to find out what thirty-six twenty means. Pack your bag."

Chapter Eleven

"Thirty-six twenty." Olivia read the numbers spotlighted on the front of Gabe's building in downtown Kansas City as he pulled into the parking garage beside the remodeled textile factory that had been turned into condominiums.

Thirty-six twenty. The street address to Gabe's building.

"Ron Kober hired someone to find out where you live?"

"I've been thinking about that. I'm in the book. My name is in the newspaper. I'm easy to find." He parked his SUV and got out, circling around to her side as she climbed down. "But Dani never listed this place as her residence. She had an apartment over in Independence in her name that we were waiting for the lease to run out on. I'm guessing that finding a dead woman's old address might require a little research." When Olivia opened the back door to retrieve her overnight bag, Gabe was there first. "I've got it."

"I'm not an invalid."

He slipped the bag over his shoulder, away from her grasping fingers, and shut the car door. "Look, the caveman in me is screaming to lock you up someplace far away from KC to keep you safe. I'm at least going to carry your damn bag."

"I guess that *is* a thing with us now," she teased. But he wasn't laughing.

With her cheek bandaged and her left arm back in its sling, Olivia felt a bit like that little girl her father and brothers still wanted to protect. Gabe, at least, hadn't argued—much—about her taking the time to change into jeans so she could wear a belt to holster her gun before coming here. She could at least concede his concern and give him credit for respecting her need for independence.

As they walked out of the parking garage, she tucked her hand into the crook of his elbow and fell into step beside him. As soon as she made the contact, he exhaled a deep breath, the tight line of his mouth relaxed and they were a team again. "Why was Kober looking for Dani?" she speculated out loud. "If he was her informant, he'd already have contact information on her, wouldn't he?"

Gabe shrugged. "I guess we can't ask him, can we."

They strolled down the sidewalk, both of their gazes looking up and down and across the street, watching for signs of any other sort of danger lurking in the alleyways and shadows. "I'll call Zeiss Security first thing in the morning. Although I hate that I have to wait until tomorrow to move forward on the case."

She nodded to the two tanklike detectives pulling up in front of the building to keep an eye on things tonight. With Jim Parker taking reports from her neighbors and reassuring them that the speeding car and gunshots were a singular incident and that they were no longer in danger, Max and Trent had volunteered to follow them up to the City Market district where Gabe lived.

If nothing else, Olivia felt that her home was safe and that the perp in the black car wouldn't try anything else tonight. It felt good to have a team of coworkers she could rely on again. Men who made her feel like an equal, not an idiot. Intellectually, she'd known all along that they were supposed to have her back, but it was a special boost to her confidence to truly believe that her evolving relationship with the cold case team meant Jim and Max and Trent, and even Katie Rinaldi and Ginny Rafferty-Taylor, were becoming real friends. They cared that she'd been threatened, and like a family—like her family—they were there for her, without any questions asked, without any games to play, without any inappropriate feelings or harassment to make her second-guess their words or actions.

By the time Gabe had shown her into his spacious loft, Olivia was feeling a lot more like her old self, a lot more like the cop she'd been destined to be from the start. He seemed to be more in his element, too, more of that mature alpha male used to being in control of his domain. The industrial look of the condo suited Gabe, with its exposed brick walls and painted pipes running across the high ceiling. The dark wood floors led into the kitchen, bathroom and living area he showed her. There was no feminine touch anywhere, giving any indication that Danielle Reese had once lived here with him.

But then he led her into a bedroom and opened up the bottom drawer of a dresser where she saw a scrap of lace, a small stuffed bear and pastel-colored items that could only suit a woman's taste. "Maybe you don't have to wait until morning to work on the investigation." He paused for a moment, squatting down to finger the lace trim that looked as though it had come from a wedding veil or gown. "If Kober was coming here to retrieve something he gave Dani, or was looking for a clue to finding the flash drive, it'd be in here."

Olivia squeezed his shoulder beside her as he walked back through the memories he'd shared with the woman he'd loved and lost. She ignored the pang of jealousy that squeezed her heart. She was smart enough to know she couldn't compete with a dead woman for Gabe's affection, or presume to take Danielle's place. If there was going to be something between her and Gabe, Olivia would forge her own place in his life. Still, she couldn't help but be a little envious of the commitment Gabe still showed to his late fiancée. If Marcus had possessed even half of Gabe Knight's integrity and devotion, he wouldn't have followed his lusty roving eye and given up on their relationship quite so easily.

She pulled away to hug her arm around her middle. Okay, so maybe it did hurt to be this close to Gabe, to want him to love her as deeply and faithfully as he had Dani, to know he was exactly the man her heart needed—and worry that, once again, her love wouldn't be enough to make the relationship work. *She* wouldn't be enough.

Love? Her love? When had that happened? When had she given her heart to cynical Mr. Caveman there?

Olivia swallowed the surprising, fearful truth that suddenly stuck in her throat. She turned away and crossed the room, giving them both the space they needed. "You don't have to show me her things, Gabe."

Shaking his head, he pulled the drawer all the way out and carried it to the bed. "Maybe Leland Asher was putting pressure on Kober to ensure no trace of Dani's story could ever get out."

Right. Talk about work. Always a much safer topic than her emotions. "Or maybe he needed her story as insurance." She came back to the foot of the bed to stand beside him. "If he released it to the public or the authorities, Asher would be screwed."

"And Senator McCoy's campaign would be over."

"Kober could have wanted it for blackmail," she pointed out.

Pulling back the front of his jacket, Gabe propped his hands at his waist. "He'd still have to find it first."

"And now that he's dead, no one's looking."

"Except for us." Gabe glanced over the jut of his shoulder at her. "That's why Asher threatened you. He wants to stop the investigation."

The whole peeping Tom thing still didn't sit right with her. A man like Leland Asher was an in-your-face kind of threat guy. The man at her window who'd run away from both her gun and the fire didn't feel like the kind of thug Asher would hire to intimidate her. Setting that conundrum aside for now, Olivia concentrated on the private investigator angle. "And you have no clue where Dani would have hidden that flash drive or any other copy of her story?"

"I've checked her jewelry box, her bank box, her desk and locker at the paper. I've asked her folks." With a weary sigh, Gabe scrubbed his hand over the late-night shadow on his cheeks and jaw before gesturing to the drawer. "This is all I've kept of her stuff. I sent the rest back to her parents. But they let me pick out a few things."

Olivia nudged aside the teddy bear to pick up the worn leather bound book beneath it. "Her diary?"

"Those entries are the last thing she ever wrote." Olivia traced the embossed name on the bottom corner of the front cover, suspecting that Gabe had given the book to Danielle Reese. "She talks about the wedding plans in there, so her mother thought I should have it."

Heavy sentimental stuff. "No notes on her story, though?"

"She never mentions a name in there except mine."

Olivia butted her shoulder against his in a sympathetic gesture. "I'm sorry."

"Don't be. I've moved beyond that part of Dani's and my story. I just need the truth." He leaned over to press a lingering kiss to her temple before pulling away and shaking off some unseen burden. "Look at anything in the drawer you want. If you can find something that helps crack this case, I don't care how personal it is, you won't hurt my feelings." He tugged the loose silk tie from beneath his collar and stuffed it into his chest pocket, dismissing himself. "Og needs to change out of this suit."

"Good," she teased, turning to watch him as he backed out the door, taking his cue to lighten the mood. "I was tired of you looking prettier than I do."

"Not possible." Those deep blue eyes that had such a talent for noticing details raked over her from head to toe and back, pausing long enough in a couple of places to make her wonder if the heat in his condo had suddenly kicked on. "The front door's bolted. The windows are locked. Your buddies are downstairs keeping an eye on things. Please don't leave this condo to chase any black cars or follow up any leads on your own while I'm in the shower."

"I won't."

Although his nod didn't look as if he was quite convinced she'd stay put, he walked out the door. "Then make yourself at home."

THE COLD SHOWER hadn't helped much.

Gabe's thoughts and his fears and his needs were full with the image of one woman…and it wasn't Dani.

He toweled his hair dry and stepped out of the master bath to pull a T-shirt on over his jeans. The clock beside his bed read well past midnight, but he wasn't tired. He was itchy inside his skin, eager to satisfy this hunger he felt around Olivia Watson that was emotional as much as it was physical. The guilt he felt at letting Dani die, at not being able to lay her memory to rest, didn't seem to affect this powerful draw he felt toward Olivia the way it had with other women he'd met since losing his fiancée.

He knew the symptoms. He was falling in love. But he was a different man than he'd been when he'd fallen for Dani. Olivia was a different woman. She was his equal in so many ways. He'd been the experienced one in his relationship with Dani. He'd tutored her in the ways of making love and breaking stories. But there wasn't anything about hard knocks and heartbreaks and digging for the truth and sharing passion he could teach Olivia. He just had to hang on for the ride and pray she wanted to be on it with him.

Gabe tossed his towel into the hamper and raked his fingers through his damp hair, debating for about two seconds before he marched out of the bedroom to seek her out.

His type-A personality wasn't going to give this a rest until he did something about it. Maybe he just needed another look at her. Maybe if he could see one more time that Leland Asher and his thugs hadn't found her, he'd be able to relax enough to get some sleep without worrying about where this relationship might or might not be going.

She hadn't moved much. Gabe paused in the open

doorway to the guest bedroom. He rubbed at the tension knotting the back of his neck, wondering if this gut-kick of reaction stirring inside his chest and behind his zipper whenever he got that first glimpse of her would go away if they did manage to stay together for a while after this case was solved. He wondered if Olivia did relationships anymore, after that idiot ex of hers had cheated on her. Hell, he wondered if he had any business trying to make something work with a KCPD cop.

Olivia was in the middle of the bed in a gray tank top and jeans. The lamps on either side of the bed bathed her skin in a golden glow and warmed the deep rich brown of her hair. She sat pretzel-style, with her sling, flannel shirt and running shoes tossed on the floor, and her gun, badge, phone and keys in a pile on the bedside table. But she'd placed the items from the drawer in a neat circle on the bed around her.

"You're staring."

"I'm enjoying the view." Her cheeks heated to a rosy pink as she refastened the back of the framed photograph she'd opened and laid it gently on the quilt beside her. "And I'm wondering if your shoulder hurts as bad as it looks."

She tugged the strap of her shirt aside to look at the fist-size bruise there. "I won't be doing push-ups for a while, but it doesn't hurt right now." Her gaze came up to meet his and she swallowed. Gabe followed the tiny ripple of movement along her creamy neck and felt his own mouth go dry. "Um. I hope this is okay." She touched the picture frame, apologizing. "I was checking to see if Dani had tucked a note inside or written on the back of the photo. You said to make myself at home. I haven't found anything useful yet."

While he appreciated her reverence to the mementos

from his past life, he was more concerned by the angry mark on her cheek and the shadows of fatigue beneath her beautiful eyes. "We can move these things out to the coffee table if you want to sleep in the guest room."

"Do you want me in the guest room?"

"I want you in my bed." His wry laugh jarred the quiet inside the room. "Is that too honest?"

Unwinding her long legs, Olivia dropped them over the edge of the bed and stood. "You can't be too honest with me, Gabe."

"But I don't want you thinking that's the only reason I brought you here." He watched her cross the room toward him. He gripped the door frame on either side to keep from reaching out to grab her and end this torment. "As long as I can see you or hold you and know you're safe—as long as you don't sneak out of here without me, you can sleep wherever you want."

But he'd forgotten the part about being equals, about Olivia being a woman with a definite mind of her own. Keeping her gaze locked onto his, she sidled right up to him, winding her arms around his waist and pressing the sleek line of her thighs and hips against his. "Is this close enough?"

Gabe's knuckles whitened on the door frame and he groaned as every male cell in his body jumped to attention at the warm friction between their bodies. "Close enough for what?"

"To keep an eye on me."

Surrendering to her game, Gabe released his grip on the door frame and stroked his fingers through the velvety softness of her hair, framing her face between them. He dipped his head and brushed a gentle kiss beside the scrape on her cheek. "No. It's not."

"How much closer can a woman get?" She stretched up to nip her teeth against his chin. "Closer?"

He turned his lips to meet hers briefly when she kissed the corner of his mouth. His heart pounded against his ribs in anticipation. "Are you sure about this?"

Her stuttering breath whispered across his lips. "I want to be closer to you, Gabe."

If they both wanted this, he wasn't going to say no. He drew his hands down her back and slipped them beneath her shirt, finding the hot, smooth skin that his hands wanted to touch. At her soft gasp, he greedily pulled her strong body against his. Her small, pert breasts pillowed against his harder chest, spearing him with twin beads of answering desire. He turned his hands, sliding his fingertips beneath the waistband of her jeans to tease the curve of her bottom. The bold minx mimicked the same action, sliding her hands inside his jeans and shorts to pull at his backside.

"Skin on skin. I like it." He dipped his mouth toward hers. "I'd like it better if it was skin inside skin."

Her breathless need mingled with his own. "Show me."

When Gabe claimed Olivia's mouth, she was right there with him. Her tongue slid against his in a feverish caress. Her lips welcomed, took, softening beneath the assault of his mouth, then demanding a firmer touch. She suckled his lower lip between hers, rubbed her silken skin against his rougher jaw. The moans in her throat matched the needy hum in his chest.

They broke apart for mere moments to peel off shirts and toss them aside. Their lips reunited first, hungry for more of each other's kisses. They shared a quick laugh when their hands reached for the snap of each other's jeans, and they each gasped at the brush of fingers against their sensitized skin. Gabe backed into the main room so they had more space to explore and touch and taste, and Olivia followed. His jeans were hanging from his hips, his erection tenting the front of his boxers when he heard an urgent, guttural excitement in her throat and moved his lips to the tempting spot.

Olivia's hands roamed over his chest and back, into his hair and over his rump, exciting every place she touched, setting his blood on fire. Gabe worked his lips against the bundle of nerves beneath her ear as he unhooked her bra.

He could barely catch his breath as he fondled her, and the proud tips strained against his palms. She tipped her head back and he kissed his way down her neck to the soft swell of her breast, teasing the tender skin with his beard, soothing it with his tongue. When he reached the pink, pebbled tip, he curled his tongue around it and drew it into his mouth, making her fingers clench against his scalp. He repeated the decadent feast on the other breast, her fingers digging through his hair, holding his mouth against her as she gasped beside his ear. "Gabe..."

"I know." His body primed to burst into flame, he scooped her up in his arms and carried her into his bedroom. He dumped her onto the dark gray bedspread, shucking off his jeans and reaching for hers as she bounced.

He paused with his hands on her hips, his chest expanding and contracting in deep, uneven breaths. "Too caveman?"

Olivia started kicking off her jeans herself, reaching for him. "No."

But Gabe pushed her back onto the pillows, loving the way the moonlight coming through the high windows caressed her bare skin, hating the way the shadows emphasized the marks on her face and shoulder. He sat on the edge of the bed, ignoring his own discomfort, and hooked one finger beneath the waistband of her pretty pink panties, sliding it back and forth across her belly, wanting to peel them off and put his mouth on her damp center yet holding back. "I don't want to hurt you, love."

"You're kidding me, right?" Her eyes, deep green with the passion that stung her lips and made her breasts dance with each needy breath, zeroed in on his. She sat up beside him, facing him. "Other than the fact I might die if you don't finish this, Gabriel Knight, I think I'm tough enough to see this through."

She wrapped her hand around the bulge in his shorts and Gabe lurched into her grip. How could he have forgotten, for even one moment, that Detective Olivia Watson was no shrinking violet.

Fine. He could make her crazy, too. He slipped his hand beneath her panties and palmed her moist, swollen heat. Her breathing switched to short, ragged gasps, but she held his gaze. Then he thrust a finger between her hot, wet folds and her eyes drifted shut. He moved a second finger inside her and her thighs clamped around his hand as she whimpered with pleasure.

"You're not so tough, Olivia Watson." He leaned in to kiss her bruised shoulder, promising tenderness as well as need. "But that can be our little secret."

Moments later, the last of their clothing was gone, Gabe had sheathed himself and settled between her legs. Sparks danced behind his eyes as he slowly entered her and filled her up. She raised her knees and hugged her arms around his shoulders, whispering against his ear. "Don't think for one moment that I don't want this, Gabe. That I don't want you." She hooked her heels behind his hips, inviting him to complete them both. "You are everything I need."

Gabe pulled partway out and slowly pushed inside her again. Her lips found his and he moved again, faster and faster. Together they found that timeless rhythm. Like tinder and flame, they stoked the fires of intimacy and desire. When they reached that flashpoint, Olivia buried her face against his neck and cried out his name. She exploded around him and the tremors of her climax caressed him until he could hold back no more. He roared with his release and emptied himself inside her.

Careful of her injuries, Gabe collapsed onto the bed beside her and gathered her into his arms. He pulled the cover from the edge of the bed and folded it over their sated, exhausted bodies. Within minutes, Olivia was dozing against his chest, her arm draped around his waist, their legs tangled together.

Gabe pressed a kiss to the crown of her hair and settled back against the pillow, watching the night sky through the window near the ceiling. Something cold and painful inside him unfurled and drifted away on the moonlight.

Now he felt she was safe. Now he could lay his love for Dani to rest. His heart had found new life, new desire, new hope in Olivia.

"OLIVIA!"

Olivia smiled at the deep-pitched bellow and hugged her knees up to her chest in the sunny warmth of the window seat where she'd been reading.

When Gabe came running out of the bedroom in nothing but his hastily pulled-on jeans, she smiled. "Good morning."

"I woke up and you weren't there. I thought..." He

raked his fingers through his coal-black hair that had already been rumpled by her hands and the deep sleep he'd finally fallen into after their second round of love-making. The shadow of his morning beard gave his angular cheeks and jaw a feral look. And that deep voice was a low lazy rumble now that the panic had dissipated. "Morning."

She tossed off the cream-colored afghan she'd covered up with to ward off the chill of the early morning, tucked a slip of paper into the diary as a bookmark and stood. She walked across the open loft to the kitchen area and set the book on the edge of the granite-top kitchen island. "I made coffee."

"I could use some."

But when she circled around to the counter where the coffeemaker steamed, he slipped his arm around her waist and pulled her up onto her toes for a firm kiss that was half passion left over from the night before and half reprimand for scaring him this morning. When her sock-covered feet hit the floor again, Olivia stroked her fingers along the stubbled line of his jaw in a soothing caress. The worry he'd felt when he'd awakened alone in bed still lingered in his eyes. "I'm okay. Sorry if you thought I'd left. I know you didn't get much sleep and I wanted to get to work." The fuzzy nap of her flannel shirt caught for a moment in the crisp curls of his dusky chest hair, as if telling her she needed to stay close to this man. Still, she made decisions with her brain, not some whimsical symbolism, and she moved away from his solid warmth to pour coffee into one of the mugs that she'd found in the cabinet. "Black, right?"

"Yeah."

She topped off her own mug and added a shot of milk

before pulling other breakfast items out of the fridge. "Eggs with your toast?"

"You cook?"

She swatted his arm when he joined her at the stove. "My grandpa taught me how. I actually enjoy it when I have the time." She cracked two eggs into the bubbling butter of the skillet and retrieved the spatula she'd used earlier from the sink. "Which reminds me, I called my dad and brothers this morning to let them know I'm still okay. Duff and Keir are on their way over to spell Max and Trent, so they can get some sleep."

That hadn't been the most pleasant of conversations. While her father was relieved to hear she hadn't been seriously injured by the driver who'd tried to run her down, he'd taken a long, fatherly pause when she told him she had stayed the night with Gabe. *Is he treating you all right, Livvy?*

A hundred percent better than Marcus ever did.

Well, he's no standard to measure a man by.

Dad, I think you'd like Gabe if you had the chance to get to know him without Danielle Reese's murder coming between you. She'd held her breath for a moment before adding, *The two of you are actually a lot alike.*

Uh-huh. He'd dismissed the possibility of him and Gabe ever burying the hatchet and getting along, and taken care of the business she'd asked about. *I'll call your brothers or come over myself if they can't make it. You don't go anywhere by yourself until we sort this out. Understand?*

I do. Thanks, Dad. I love you.

"Liv?"

She snapped her thoughts back to the present and quickly flipped the eggs before the yolks turned to rubber. "I just wanted to reassure you that there will be someone watching us 24/7 now. Until we get this case solved and find out who owns that black car."

"What did your family say when you told them where you were?"

"Um, well..." So he knew exactly where her thoughts had wandered off to. "You do get bonus points for help-ing me last night and wanting to keep me safe. But they made it clear that they're here to protect *me*. Not you."

Gabe lifted his mug in a toast. "I can live with that."

"Don't worry, Gabe." She pulled out a plate and dished up his breakfast. "If you get caught in the cross-fire, I'll be watching your back."

"No. You're the one in danger."

"You were trapped in that fire, too. I don't think these people care who gets hurt as long as it isn't them."

"I'm not going to have you taking any extra risks be-cause of me. If Asher's men come after me, good. Let 'em come. It'll take the focus off you."

"I'm not going to let anyone..." She caught her breath, stopping the argument before it went any further. Since neither of them would budge on protecting the other, she raised her hands in a silent truce and changed the topic. "I've been reading Dani's diary."

"I saw that." Gabe stood there, a handsome, rumpled, stubborn devil, eating his breakfast. Olivia crossed to the opposite side of the kitchen island and pulled out a stool to sit. He pointed his fork at the diary when she opened it. "I don't suppose you found anything. I didn't miss her naming her informant or exactly what dirt she had on Asher and McCoy?"

Olivia flipped through the pages, remembering some of the entries there. "No. It's filled with normal things a woman writes in her diary. Falling in love. Arguments.

Concerns. Things she was looking forward to." She glanced up at Gabe. "Things that frustrated her."

He made a face and went back to eating. "Did anything jump out at you? A fresh set of eyes usually sees something new."

Dani had been planning a simple, summery, outdoor wedding at her parents' home in Kansas, with a second reception slated for the tony Cattleman's Club here in the city. She wrote about how much she had learned from Gabe as a reporter, and the new places and life experiences he'd shared with her personally. But mostly, Dani had written about falling in love, and how, no matter what, she loved being with him. "She was a talented writer. Almost poetic at times."

Gabe nodded, swallowing the last forkful of eggs. "Yet she could be completely straightforward and lose the purple prose when it came to the articles she wrote."

Dani had mentioned that, too, how Gabe had taken her raw skills and turned her into a better writer. "Some of the things she says in here, the way she says them, reminded me that a woman thinks differently than a man."

He gave her a thumbs-up on the breakfast and drank a sip of coffee. "That's not news worth reporting, Detective."

"Dani was angry that night she left."

"Yes."

"She downloaded her story and file notes onto her flash drive so you couldn't spy on her and tell her what she was doing wrong or—"

"I didn't say she was wrong. Her story was legit. I wanted her to understand that the people she was about to expose would do whatever it took to stop her. She didn't have backup who knew to go looking for her if she didn't call in or show up at a certain time. She was meeting in a dangerous part of town. She didn't have the right kind of protection in place."

As the tension radiating off him increased, Olivia reached across the island to touch his hand to soothe him. "I get it. You were both upset."

Gabe nodded, understanding that this was about piecing together a puzzle, not placing blame. He squeezed her hand before taking his plate to the sink to rinse it and put it in the dishwasher. "Sorry. That's old news. I know you're leading up to something. What is it?"

"When a woman gets really emotional like that, she has a go-to plan, a habit she uses to regain her equilibrium. Especially if she has an important job or responsibilities she has to take care of."

Gabe picked up the pan and spatula to load them into the dishwasher, as well. "Like five minutes of peace and quiet."

"That's right. Some women go for a run. Others take a bubble bath. I like to be alone in a place that's calm and serene." Like spending an hour watching the sun come up over the city skyline from the secluded nook of Gabe's window seat. She hadn't just been reading the diary, she needed some time to process the emotional upheaval of sleeping together and realizing just how important he'd become to her in the short span of time they'd been together. But that was a discussion for another time. "Where did Dani go when you two had a fight?"

"We didn't fight that much."

Olivia waved aside his defensive argument. "When anything upset her or frustrated her, what was her go-to plan to cool off and compose herself?"

Gabe finished his task and closed the dishwasher, using the time to think before rejoining her at the island.

"She liked to go up onto the roof. She planted some flower boxes and a bunch of pots with herbs on the deck up there, bought some patio furniture and a grill. She kept saying one day when we stopped working we were going to have friends over and entertain up there."

"You probably hated the idea of not working."

"So did she." He smiled at the fond memory. "But she'd plug in some music and go up there to trim off dead blooms, put together bouquets and dig around in the dirt."

Dani had been murdered on a rainy autumn night. "Would she go up there even if the weather wasn't nice?"

Gabe nodded. "She built a snowman up there once."

"Are the pots and flower boxes still up there?"

"She went up there that night. I swear I could hear her cursing through the ceiling. She went down the fire escape and left without coming back in to say goodbye." Gabe's hands fisted on the cool granite. "And I was too proud or angry or whatever stupid emotion I was feeling to go up there and apologize. I thought she'd come back down and we'd have a civilized discussion about how to handle her story."

Blame and regret didn't matter right now. Olivia climbed down off the stool. "How do I get to the roof?"

Gabe's blue eyes locked onto hers and widened. "Are you saying finding that flash drive is that easy?"

Olivia hurried into the guest bedroom where she'd left her tennis shoes and shouted her answer. "Not exactly easy. We haven't actually found it yet. And it might not be there. Six years have passed. You and my dad searched in the places a man would think of. Logical places. This is just a hunch I have based on…"

When she came back out with her shoes on, Gabe had disappeared. Seconds later, he walked out of his room, buttoning a starched blue shirt over the T-shirt he'd put on. "I'd trust your hunches over most people's eyewitness testimony any day, Detective." He pulled on socks and shoes, grabbed his keys and reached for her hand. "Let's go look."

Six years with mostly Mother Nature to take care of the rooftop garden had turned the red paint on the deck railings and flower boxes brown. The only flowers that had survived since their last caretaker were a pair of overgrown rosebushes in two giant pots chained to the railing at the far end of the deck. Dani had chosen hardy plants because, even now, there were new green shoots pushing up through the dirt.

"I can see why she'd like it up here." Olivia squinted into the damp morning breeze that indicated they'd have rain later in the day. But the view up here was panoramic, with the tallest buildings of downtown KC far enough away that she could see for miles in almost any direction. She tried for a few moments to think like Dani would have that night. "Are there any lights up here?"

Gabe nodded. "She used to string party lights up here. But you have to turn them on…" He paused to unlock a small shed. "In here." He hit a switch, turning on a bare lightbulb hanging in the middle of the shed, as well as twin spotlights on the outside, angled over the deck area. "That's the light she would have had that night, plus a few twinklers hanging from the railings."

"It's not much." She followed him inside the shed after he moved aside a grill and deck chairs stored there, clearing a path.

"It would have been crowded like this in here, too," Gabe added, uncovering the grill and checking inside. "We packed everything up over Labor Day weekend."

"Then it needed to be a place she could get to quickly. She wasn't up here that long, right?"

"Maybe five minutes, tops."

"Are there any cabinets or storage boxes where she might have stashed the flash drive?" Olivia asked, drifting toward the wall display of a couple dozen colorful glazed pots that Gabe or someone had brought inside out of the elements.

"Just those open shelves and the stuff sitting around on the floor." He pulled out a galvanized bucket and set it on the floor beside her. "We can use this or the empty pots to dump the dirt into and sift through it if you think it's in one of those."

The dirt inside the pots was dry and cracked or had filtered through the disintegrating bases of some to form neat, pyramid-shaped piles on the floor and shelves. She picked up a turquoise pot to start the search. Wait. Not so neat. She recognized the tracks through the dirt where tiny feet and balancing tails had scurried through.

Her heart thumped rapidly in her chest as she stepped back. "Do you have mice in here?"

"I'm sure they come in during the wintertime. Do you want me to search in here and you take the flower boxes?"

"No." Inhaling a quieting breath, she turned the pot upside down and shook the globs of solidified potting soil into the bucket. "I'm a professional cop and a grown… Yes!" A tiny black mouse landed in the bucket and Olivia screamed. The turquoise pot shattered on the concrete floor as the vile little vermin froze for a moment, looking up to see who'd disturbed his hiding place. Then he darted away as fast as Olivia dashed back onto the deck.

"Easy, tough lady." Gabe caught her in the middle of the deck and pulled her into his arms. "Hey. You're shaking."

A dozen different curses went through Olivia's head. She hated this weakness. And though she wanted to be able to shake it off and deal with this on her own, she found herself clutching a handful of Gabe's shirt and leaning against his shoulder instead. "Dad said my mother was terrified of mice, too. I think it's a hereditary thing. Don't think my brothers didn't take advantage of that one." But the firm stroke of Gabe's fingers at the nape of her neck took the edge off her irrational fear, and allowed her to think and breathe normally again. If a kid with a knife and gun and a man in a speeding black car couldn't scare her away from this investigation, then no furry little rodent would, either. "I'm okay." She pressed a kiss to the edge of Gabe's jaw and pushed away. "I'm okay."

"I'm just glad you're not so independent you don't need me for something," he teased, although the humor didn't quite reach his eyes. He turned away and went back into the shed.

It was on the tip of her tongue to call him back and tell him that she needed him to make her whole again. She needed him to love her and teach her to believe in trust and her own judgment and happy futures again. She just needed him. Of all the crazy possibilities in the world, she needed Gabe Knight, the one man in all of KC who hadn't broken the law, who didn't like cops. She needed him.

She loved him.

"I'll face the beast in here. If I find something, I'll bring it out." When he stepped back outside a few seconds later, Olivia shook the distracting revelation from her head. He set a pair of women's gardening gloves and a small hand shovel in her hands. "Here. Take these if you're going to be digging through the dirt."

"Thanks."

Ignoring her troublesome thoughts and wary heart for now, Olivia pulled on the gloves and started poking through the dirt and peeking through the slats at her feet. Common sense sent her to the flower boxes on either side of the railing where they'd entered off the fire escape. If Dani hadn't had much time to hide the flash drive, she would have looked for the most convenient place—if she'd hidden it up here at all. Olivia scooted the dirt around and dug all the way down to the wood at the bottom. Nothing.

Olivia sighed in frustration, scanning the nearly empty deck. She'd thought she was onto something here. This place was secluded, had limited access to outsiders, and it was probably the place where Dani had felt the safest. It's where Olivia would have stashed the flash drive for safekeeping until she could retrieve it later. But would Dani have done the same?

Even with the overcast sky, the morning sun had masked the most obvious hiding place of all. Olivia looked at the spotlight on the shed, and looked again. Her pulse rate kicked up a notch, with a far more even, healthier excitement than the startle she'd gotten from her run-in with Mighty Mouse.

"Are you sentimental about any of these flowers?" she shouted to Gabe, following the beam of the right spotlight over to one of the potted rosebushes.

"No." He came to the door as she plunged her shovel into the pot, attacking the base of the bush to loosen up the soil. "Did you find something?"

"She was up here at night, for just a few minutes. She

needed to catch her breath, clear her mind and hide her story so that she could get to the appointment with her informant on time."

"That light shines right on this pot." He joined her, pulling away the dirt with his gloved hands, then grasping the stalks of the plant itself, tugging and twisting until the roots started to give way. "She wouldn't have had to take time to unlock the shed, and she would have been able to see what she was doing here."

A big chunk of the gnarled old bush pulled free, dumping a shower of dirt at their feet. Gabe dumped the plant onto the deck and reached in to pull the rest of it out. But there was no need. Olivia dug out clumps of the broken roots and sifted through the dirt and debris with her gloved fingers. Was that… She felt the crinkle of something nonorganic between the root ball and the side of the pot.

"Gabe?" She yanked the zipped-up plastic bag from its hiding place. "Gabe!"

"Is that what I think it is?"

She brushed six years of dirt and the elements off the bag and held it up to the spotlight. Olivia was almost giddy with relief when they saw what was inside.

A thumb-size flash drive attached to a silver key ring.

"That's Dani's," Gabe confirmed, pressing a kiss to Olivia's cheek. "You found it."

"If the weather hasn't destroyed it completely, our lab can do amazing things."

He pulled off their gloves and tossed them and the tool into the shed and locked the door. "What are we waiting for?"

Olivia nodded and hurried down the stairs ahead of him. "Who's waiting?"

Chapter Twelve

"I know who murdered Danielle Reese."

Olivia stood at the side of the table and looked around at her team. Other than Gabe, who'd been at the crime lab with her yesterday and had read the same files recovered from the flash drive they'd found, she was met with looks that ranged from mild surprise to disbelief.

Max leaned back in his chair, blurting out what the others must have been thinking. "Then why don't we have this guy in custody? What's the catch?"

It was a big one. "I'm not sure I can prove it."

Ginny Rafferty-Taylor quieted her office by simply raising her hand. "Maybe you'd better give us a little more explanation. We all know how rare it is to get a confession on a cold case. Do you have circumstantial evidence?"

"Yes, ma'am. A ton of it." Olivia turned her laptop around to pull up the list of files she'd copied from the flash drive. She put it up on the screen behind her for everyone to read. "Dani Reese was meticulous about documenting her research."

"If I may?" Gabe sat at the table now, too. He'd been accepted as an integral part of this investigation if not exactly welcomed as friend. "Dani kept photos of corroborating evidence and transcripts of interviews with her informant, as well as several drafts of the articles she was writing about Leland Asher making payoffs to Adrian McCoy's campaign in exchange for political favors such as rezoning property Asher wanted or adjusting funding programs that would benefit his legitimate businesses or cutting budgets so there would be fewer cops in the neighborhoods where he conducts his less legitimate enterprises."

"Money laundering. Drug trafficking. Racketeering," Trent added. "We know the list. That flash drive can prove Leland Asher is a crook?"

Olivia answered. "We found evidence of collusion, at least. Although we can't tie him directly to Dani Reese's murder."

Max frowned. "I thought you said he killed that poor lady."

Olivia was quick to clarify. "I didn't say it was Asher. But whether she intended to or not, Dani did tell us who shot her that night."

"So what did she say?" Max asked. "What secrets are on that flash drive?"

"Dani used an old-school reporting technique," Gabe jumped in, explaining the gold mine of information the crime lab had retrieved from his late fiancée's notes. "She documented activities before and after each meeting. Basically, she kept a logbook to record her research, make note of potential sidebars, keep track of all the details of who, what, when and where, in case it might be related to her main story." He gestured to Olivia, throwing their attention back to her. "That's where we picked up on the man Olivia is talking about."

Olivia opened one of the files. "He must have been stalking her for several days, if not weeks before the murder. She mentions him several times."

Lieutenant Rafferty-Taylor jotted a note on the pad in front of her. "Stalking? Did Ms. Reese have contact with him? Had he threatened her before that night?"

"Not directly." Olivia punched a button on her laptop to post an image up on the screen. "Here's an example of one entry." She read Dani's words out loud.

"He never talks to me. But today he followed me through the park when I was power walking with Lucy after lunch. I think he has a crush and is just too shy to approach me. I've seen him in line at the coffee shop, parked in his car at the grocery store, pumping gas when I filled up my tank yesterday. But I don't know his name. He just watches me. He sneaks closer when he thinks I'm not looking. This guy gives me the creeps."

Katie Rinaldi shivered. "It'd give me the creeps, too, to have some guy lurking around me like that." When Trent reached over to squeeze her shoulder, she smiled and went back to work. "Did she happen to give a name to this scumbag so I can put him in the case file and we can track him down?"

"No name, but she gave a good description of him in several different places in her reports. Reddish-brown hair. Slight build." Olivia posted a collage of candid photos. "She even gave us his picture."

Several of them, in fact. A skinny guy waiting for a table on the far side of a coffee shop, his face partly obscured by the crowd of patrons between them. The same man in a hooded sweatshirt, caught at an awkward angle as though Dani Reese had been trying to hide the fact she was taking a picture. A young man sitting in a beat-up car across the street from the *Journal*'s parking garage.

"According to the time stamp on the photos, these were all taken in the two weeks before she died."

Max sat up in his chair and snapped his fingers. "Hey. I know that guy."

Gabe pulled back his sleeve and raised his arm to point to the gauze bandage covering the stitches there. "We all do."

"You're talking about Stephen March." Max smacked Trent on the arm beside him. "Son of a gun. We had that kid in here yesterday. He was high as a kite. He's the one who left his DNA on Mr. Reporter there."

Jim Parker took his cue from Olivia's nod and passed out copies of Stephen March's DMV photo and vehicle registration. "Five bucks if anyone can guess what kind of car Stephen March drives now."

"Black Dodge Challenger?" Gabe drawled.

Jim nodded. "He's been following Liv the same way he followed Dani Reese—maybe learning her routine and looking for the opportunity to find her alone, maybe working up the nerve to strike again."

Gabe set the papers on the table. "That's the car I saw try to run down Olivia. The last three digits of the license plate number are the same."

"And I saw the same car speeding away from the warehouse fire." Olivia nodded to her partner to continue.

"I talked to March at his sister's house after leaving your place," Jim said. "Found the car there, too, parked out back. One of the taillights was missing and the hood was still warm so I know he hadn't been watching TV down in the basement like he claimed. His sister looked too much like the family-sedan type to have been racing

around in that thing. He couldn't account for his whereabouts the night of the fire, either. 'Out looking for some
friends' isn't much of an alibi."

"The sister wouldn't confirm his alibi?" the lieutenant asked.

Jim shook his head. "She said the basement apartment has a separate entrance, and she doesn't always
know when he comes and goes. In fact, she didn't say
much at all. She seemed so skittish about having a cop
in the house with her that I did the interview out on the
front porch."

"She sounds like a piece of work," Max grumbled.

"Nonetheless," Ginny interrupted, "we have a viable
suspect. Where is Mr. March now?"

Max shoved his chair away from the table and
stood. "Hell. I'm an idiot. He's in holding. Yesterday,
we booked him for assault and illegal possession of a
firearm. He probably thinks he dodged a bullet because
we didn't mention murder. You want me to bring him
up here for questioning?"

"Hold on, Max." The lieutenant looked up at Olivia,
her keen blue eyes seeing that even her lead detective
didn't think this was a slam-dunk case yet. "What else
do we need to prove he's our guy?"

"Motive would be nice. Most stalkers know their victims. As far as I can tell, Stephen and Dani were only
random acquaintances who frequented the same businesses for the last two weeks of her life. There's no evidence that he issued any kind of threat. And she never
reported him to the police."

Ginny followed up with a question to Gabe. "And
Ms. Reese never mentioned this alleged stalker to you?"

Olivia recognized the grim line of Gabe's mouth and
the guilt it represented. He shook his head. "She didn't

tell me anything about the story she was working on or anything about that…undercover part of her life. I didn't know what was going on until I read her notes." He raked his fingers through his hair, erasing some of the tension and leaving a sea of rumpled spikes in their wake. "Are you sure he wasn't working for Leland Asher?" Gabe proposed for the umpteenth time since they'd reviewed Dani's research together. "That this whole stalking setup isn't some kind of cover-up for Asher's involvement?"

Olivia wanted to believe that, too. Lord knew there was plenty of information on that flash drive that Asher wouldn't want the authorities to know about. "The evidence doesn't support that. We have no proof that the two men have ever even met. They certainly don't run in the same social circles or live in the same neighborhood. And there's no record anywhere of money changing hands between them. Unless March gives him up when we interview him, there's no way to link Asher to the actual murder."

Trent Dixon interjected another voice of reason. "According to his juvie record and stints in rehab, that kid has been doped out of his mind for half his life. If Ms. Reese smiled at him or shared a casual conversation, that might have been all it took for him to believe there was a connection between them. If he finally worked up the nerve to approach her that night, and she didn't reciprocate…"

Olivia agreed. Reluctantly. "I know that's happened before. I still think there has to be a connection between Asher and Dani Reese beyond her uncovering a story on him. But right now, all the circumstantial evidence points to Stephen March having acted alone."

"Don't worry, Liv," the lieutenant reassured her. "Leland Asher isn't going to walk away from this unscathed." She turned to the brunette taking notes on her computer. "Katie—I want you to copy this to your uncle in the DA's office, see if he agrees we've got enough to get an arrest warrant for Mr. Asher."

Katie nodded. "Detectives Hendricks and Kincaid, too?"

"Yes."

"Sawyer and Joe will want to reinterview Elaine Kober." Olivia tapped her own laptop, indicating Dani's files. "And Zeiss Security. The *E* on the note Mr. Kober tried to get rid of stood for Elaine. When I talked to their representative, he said Ron Kober hired them to investigate his wife's 'suspicious' activities. Apparently, he wanted a divorce so he could marry his assistant, Misty Harbison, but with his infidelity track record, he needed some ammunition or else he'd be paying Elaine big bucks."

Gabe had been as surprised as she was when they'd read the notations in Dani's files. "For years now, I assumed Ron Kober was BB, Dani's informant." He shook his head, admitting his mistake. "But it was Ron's wife. Dani's first draft of her story uses the feminine pronouns *she* and *her*. Later, she changed them to genderless references to protect her source. Elaine was at almost every public event and private party her husband was. She'd be privy to what went on behind the scenes."

Olivia opened another file and put it up on the screen. "Elaine Kober took these pictures and gave them to Dani." There was a photo of a check signed by Leland Asher, sitting on top of several stacks of cash in Ron Kober's office during his tenure working for Senator McCoy. The paperwork beside it showed the check had been counted as a campaign contribution, but not the cash. Another picture showed Asher whispering into McCoy's ear at a charity event, with her husband lurking in the background. "I think she was more interested in exposing her husband's criminal activities as payback for his continued infidelity than she was with any sense of civic duty."

"And he didn't find out about her betrayal until now?" Katie asked.

"Or, he overlooked it." Olivia had a theory about that seriously twisted relationship, too. "Their divorce would have been expensive and messy. If Ron Kober could find that missing flash drive, he could hand it over to Leland Asher and let his old 'business associate' take care of the problem one way or another. I'm guessing Elaine found out what he was up to, there was an ugly argument and it ended with her bashing him in the head."

Max let out a low whistle. "Sheesh. That's why I'm never getting married."

"You're never getting married because no smart woman would have you," Trent gibed. "When we interviewed Stephen March, he said he saw a blonde woman cleaning in Kober's office—that's why he didn't stay to rob the place. We can show him pictures, including Mrs. Kober's, and see if he picks her out of a lineup."

Max laughed, not minding being the butt of his partner's joke. "What a loser. He went there to kill Kober, but the wife beat him to it. No wonder he freaked out on you two."

Olivia slipped back into her chair, not feeling the morbid laughter in the room. "That's the part that doesn't sit right with me. If March was stalking Dani, and she rejected him or did something else to send him over the edge into violence, then what's his motive for going after Kober?" She shook her head. "Even if he was there for drugs or money like he claims, it's an awfully big coincidence for him to show up at the scene of two related murders six years apart." She met Gabe's gaze across the table. She knew he felt the same. They'd solved the case, had solved three crimes, in fact, by the time others in KCPD rounded up Leland Asher and Elaine Kober. But the puzzle wasn't complete yet. "I just feel like there's something more going on here."

"Let's not borrow trouble. We've got a solid case against March." Their team leader wasn't about to let a murderer go because Olivia's instincts were nagging at her. "The gun you took off March and the gun you found in the warehouse are both the same make and caliber. A Raven Arms MP25. I know it's not conclusive, but criminals do tend to repeat themselves. It certainly builds more and more of a circumstantial case against him." Ginny rose from her seat at the head of the table, making a command decision. "Let's bring March up here and lay our case on the table—see if he feels like talking."

While Max and Trent stood to put on jackets and gather their notepads and laptops, Katie read an email off her computer screen. "I've already got a reply from Detective Kincaid. He and his partner are on their way to visit Mrs. Kober now."

"Hold up, gentlemen." Lieutenant Rafferty-Taylor patted Olivia's shoulder. "This is your case. Why don't you go down to holding and tell Stephen March the good news—that in addition to assaulting you and Mr. Knight, we're booking him for Dani Reese's murder. Good work, everyone."

Olivia followed the older woman to her desk. "Is it all right if I call my father in, ma'am? He was the original detective on this case. I know he'd like to be there when we finally close it."

Even if there were some loose ends about this investigation that nagged at her, Olivia knew getting a murderer off the streets was always a good thing. Helping her father find closure on an otherwise stellar career he'd been forced to end before he was ready to was even better.

The lieutenant agreed. "Make the call."

"WHAT DO YOU MEAN he's not in his cell?" Olivia turned 360 degrees, taking in the seemingly normal chaos of the holding wing's long hallway, processing counter, barred gates and steel doors beyond, as well as her father's shaking head and Gabe's piercing glare. "Where is he?"

Max was at the sergeant's desk, cursing the ineptitude of paper pushers and the stupid luck of the world in general while Trent Dixon offered a saner explanation for why the man she was here to arrest had gone missing. "March collapsed in his cell. The guard said he was going through some serious withdrawal symptoms this morning. Don't know if it's his heart or his lungs or his stomach, but he just couldn't handle detoxing cold turkey. They took him in an ambulance to Saint Luke's about an hour ago."

"Is he still alive?"

"As far as I know."

"Is he still there? Is he under guard?"

"You know he is. We're not going to let this guy slip through our fingers again." Curling his mouth into a wry grin, Trent patted Olivia's shoulder and excused himself. "Why don't you go down to Saint Luke's and read him his rights yourself while I take care of Mr. Charm School over there before he gets put on report."

"Thanks, Trent."

The big man nodded. "We'll follow as soon as we can."

"Gabe? Dad? Jim? Let's go."

Jim dangled his keys in front of her and backed toward the exit. "I'll drive."

Jim put the siren on the roof of his extended cab pickup, and got them to the downtown hospital in a matter of minutes. But the deathly quiet from the back seat Gabe shared with her father made the ride seem to last an hour.

Still, smoothing over familial tensions and figuring out whether she and Gabe had any future beyond working together to solve this case had to be filed away and dealt with later. Right now, she had a murderer to track down and put into official custody. She and Jim flashed their badges to give their guns clearance, and all four of them quickly moved through the security checkpoint to get into the hospital.

With Trent feeding them information over the phone, they hurried through the multistory lobby, skipped the information desk and went straight to the elevators to get to the second floor. "Room 222. Thanks, Trent."

Olivia tucked her phone away in her pocket and led the way out of the elevator and around the corner into the second-floor corridor. But her steps slowed to an uneasy pace long before they reached the room at the end of the hallway. Suspicion pricked the hairs at the back of her neck. Something wasn't right.

Jim stopped beside her, sensing it, too. "I don't like this." He checked behind them, then swiveled his green-eyed gaze back along the empty corridor. "Where's the guard?"

The chair outside the door was there. But there was no one standing watch at Stephen March's room. Olivia pulled back her jacket and unsnapped her holster. Resting her hand on the butt of her weapon, she warned Gabe and her father to stay back. "Wait here."

Gabe took a step after her. "Olivia, be care—"

"Let me do my job, caveman."

With a fuming reluctance, Gabe nodded and ducked into the room next door with her father.

Nodding her readiness to Jim, they both pulled their guns and flanked the door to room 2022. Switching between guarding and taking point, they quickly cleared the room, closet and adjoining bathroom. The rumpled bed and IV tube, needle and tape still swinging from its solution bag indicated March hadn't been gone for long. The empty, unlocked ring of the handcuffs still attached to the bed's steel frame made her think he hadn't left on his own, either.

Olivia muttered one choice curse and pulled out her phone. "What is happening here? Who's helping him escape?"

Jim holstered his gun and hurried out the door. "I'll check the front desk."

"Livvy?" Thomas Watson limped out into the hallway after the all clear, with a KCPD badge in his hand. "We've got an unconscious man in here. His ID says Derek Logan. I'm guessing he's your guard."

"Pretty nasty blow to the back of the head," Gabe added. "I already called the hospital staff from the phone in the room. Told them he'd need assistance as soon as it was safe."

Olivia added the badge number to the report she was making to Dispatch. "That checks out. Whoever's helping March is going to be in street clothes or hospital gear," she added before hanging up. "Officer Logan is the guard assigned to March. So we don't know who the accomplice is. We have to look for March."

"I notified hospital security. They're sending someone to every exit point." Jim returned with a nurse who hurried into the room to attend to the injured officer. "The nurse there said she took March's vitals ten minutes ago and he was still showing signs of detox. Chills, shakes, headache. It'd be hard for him to walk out of here."

"That means he's in a wheelchair or on a gurney." That meant the elevators. Olivia cursed. "They were probably going down when we were heading up. If they get out to the parking lot before security locks this place down, we'll never catch them."

Gabe grabbed her arm and stopped her when she hurried past. Any instinct to argue fell silent when she saw the keen intelligence lighting his eyes. "If he's on a gurney or in a chair, then they'd have to take the staff elevators. The hospital staff would stop and question them if they tried to get on the public elevators."

Oh, how she loved that cool logic of his. "You're right. Max and Trent are on their way, too. But we need to find them now. Ten minutes isn't that much of a head start if they had to disable Officer Logan and sneak out of the room."

She pointed to Jim but he was already nodding, moving down the hallway, sharing the same idea. "Let's split up. I'll search this floor, make sure they're not hiding out, and you get on down to the first. Hopefully, we can at least contain him here before he reaches any of the exits."

Thomas Watson still had KCPD blue running through his veins. "Livvy, you take Knight with you. I'll stay and help Detective Parker."

"Dad, you're not armed." She glanced up at Gabe. "Neither one of you are."

"Olivia Mary, I love you to death, but if you let this guy get away…"

She winked at her father and nodded. "Yes, sir. Let's go."

Leaving her father to limp into the room across from Jim, Olivia dashed toward the staff elevators and cleared each car before running to the stairs. Gabe was already there, shoving open the door and following close behind as she charged down the empty stairs to the first floor. A quick glance down the first floor service corridor showed no men who resembled Stephen March's receding hairline and wiry build.

But Gabe's hand at the small of her back turned her attention to the orderly pushing a wheelchair out through a swinging door. The patient bundled in a blanket looked far too familiar. "They're heading out to the lobby."

"Stay behind me," she ordered, pulling her gun and breaking into a run. "Call Jim and tell him we've got them."

For once, Gabe obeyed a command. Sort of. As she paused at the swinging steel door and peeked through to make sure the path was clear, she could hear Gabe giving Jim a succinct explanation of the situation and location. But he was right on her heels as she pushed through the door. "We've got a lot of civilians down here," he added before hanging up.

"Oh, my God," Olivia whispered, lowering her weapon. The public lobby at Saint Luke's was as tricky to navigate as downtown rush hour. The carpeted area was a maze of chair groupings, sculptures and planters filled with trees and flowers—not to mention the gift shop, information desk and dozens of staff, visitors and volunteers crossing through and hanging out there. "Do you see them?"

She and Gabe stood back-to-back, turning, searching. Wrong color hair. Too tall. A woman in that wheelchair. No orderly with that one. There was still only one guard at the front glass doors.

She felt Gabe's firm grip on her elbow and turned. "There. That's him."

Olivia moved out in a quick walk, keeping the orderly wearing green scrubs in her line of sight as she darted from one chair to the next tree. The patient in the wheelchair was bundled up with blankets that masked most of his face, but the shaking hands holding the covers up to his nose were a dead giveaway. The pair headed for the glass doors away from the check-in station at a fast enough clip that the guard had noticed them, too.

She held up her badge and waved him back, angling her head toward the families and staff, hoping he understood her silent request to start moving people away from the doors and the potential confrontation.

And then she saw the bulge in the back of the green scrubs. March's accomplice was no orderly. He was carrying a gun.

"Gabe?" She glanced up, sharing her concern with the man who never seemed to miss a detail.

He saw it, too. He squeezed her arm and started moving toward a seating area where two children were putting together a puzzle. "I'll get as many people out of here as I can."

There was a matter of yards between her and the two escapees when a woman screamed. She'd seen Olivia's gun.

Stephen and the orderly both glanced over their shoulders. And then they were running.

"Ah, hell." Olivia planted her feet and raised her weapon and Gabe whisked the hysterical woman out of harm's way. "KCPD! Stephen March! You with the wheelchair! I order you to stop."

Stephen shoved the blankets off his chair and tried to rise, but the covers tangled with the spokes of the wheel and the chair tipped over, throwing him to the floor. The man with the gun leaped over him, muttering something like, "You're on your own."

But the guard had locked the doors and when the orderly slammed into them, he knew he was trapped.

Olivia advanced. "Stop where you are. Drop your weapon."

The woman shrieked again when the man pulled his gun and spun around. "Get back!" he yelled, waving the gun back and forth before settling on her as the biggest threat in the room. "You get back!"

"Not gonna happen." Olivia froze, leveled her gun at the middle of his chest. "Everybody get down!"

"Olivia!" Gabe's warning shout was the last thing she heard as she fingered the trigger.

The next few seconds passed by in a slow-motion blur.

Stephen March crawled out of the wreckage and lurched to his feet. Olivia saw the gunman's finger squeeze the trigger. An elderly woman rose from her chair, blocking Olivia's line of sight.

"Get down!" she warned, averting her weapon and praying the gunman was a lousy shot.

There were two loud bangs from off to her left. The glass behind the perp shattered and the gunman went down.

Olivia glanced over and saw Jim Parker lowering his steaming weapon. "Told you I had your back, partner." He jogged past her and knelt beside the assailant, picking up his gun and checking the man's neck for a pulse. He shook his head as she joined him. "This one's done." He was already waving her off as she backed toward the path Stephen March had taken. "Yours is getting away. Go."

"Thanks. Partner."

The world reverted to real time as she took off after March. Even in his unsteady condition, that tweaker could fly. He knocked a man in a suit and the nurse beside him out of his way and zigzagged toward the gift shop. Alert to the danger now, the other patrons and staff dodged out of Olivia's path. He'd reached the long hallway now, stretching the distance between them. Her lungs were burning and she pressed harder. Her shoulder ached and...

A metal-rimmed chair flew across the carpet, knocking the young man off his feet.

Olivia caught a glimpse of coal-black hair as she ran past and grinned.

The man who'd escaped from lockup at the hospital— the man who'd gotten away with murder for six years, who'd tarnished her father's career, who'd tried to kill her more than once—moaned as he tried to push himself to his feet.

But Stephen March didn't take one more step. Olivia holstered her gun, put her elbow to the back of his neck and took him right back down to the ground. He groaned and complained and muttered a nervous stream of words that didn't always make sense. Olivia's voice was breathless with exertion, but perfectly clear as she pulled the handcuffs off her belt. "Stephen March, you are under arrest for the murder of Danielle Reese."

"What? I swear I didn't mean... Ah, hell. What about Rosemary? My sister needs me. I'm so sorry. I didn't mean to." He writhed on the floor beneath her knee, fidgeting with his fingers almost as soon as she pulled his hands together behind his back. He repeated the same words over and over, almost crying in his manic state. "I didn't mean to. I'm sorry. I didn't mean to."

She felt the tall shadow coming up beside her, and

recognized the familiar starchy scent as Gabe knelt beside her. "You just couldn't stay out of the way, could you?" she chided. "You didn't think I was going to run him down this time?"

"I had no doubt you were going to catch him, but this idiot doesn't get to hurt the woman I love."

A few of those words tried to reach her heart, but Olivia had to finish the job first. "Is everybody in the lobby safe?"

"Yes. Scared, but fine." He reached out beside her, pinning March's flailing legs. "You got him yet?"

"I don't know who that guy was." March's rambling never ceased. "He said he had to help me. I had to kill that girl. I had to save my sister. I didn't mean to. I didn't want—"

Olivia could seriously use five minutes of peace and quiet right now. She slapped the first cuff on his wrist. "You have the right to remain silent."

Gabe added, "I recommend using that right."

"Anything you say…" Olivia paused, seeing her father's uneven gait as he walked up on the scene, flanked by Max Krolikowski, Trent Dixon and Jim Parker. She looked up and smiled at her friends, her partner and her father. All men she could depend on, men who'd shown her time and again that they believed in her skills, that they trusted her, that she could trust them. A feeling of warmth rose up inside her, a feeling a belonging, a certainty that the damage Marcus Brower had done to her was finally in the past and that she would never have to second-guess these relationships again.

She smiled her thanks to each of them, but paused when she met Thomas Watson's moss-green eyes. She held up the loose end of the handcuffs. "Dad. This is your collar. Go ahead and close your last case."

"I'm proud of you, sweetheart." He squatted down on the other side of Stephen March and closed the cuff around the other wrist. Then the two of them helped March to his feet and finished Mirandizing him. "Your mother would be, too."

"We'll take him." Trent nodded to Olivia and her father and pulled Stephen March between him and Max. They turned with Jim and walked down the hallway to return their prisoner to lockup.

A worrisome pang tainted the satisfied feeling of success that had made everything right in her world for a few moments. She tipped her face up to Gabe. This case had brought them together. But the hunt for the truth was over. He had his answers. She'd solved the case and captured his fiancée's killer. He could finally lay his guilt to rest. What happened now? "Thank you."

His deep, hushed voice resonated in her ears. "This never would have happened without you."

The next moment was filled with awkward silence.

Until her father's gruff voice interrupted. "Oh, for Pete's sake, you two—get in an empty room and say what you need to say."

Gabe didn't argue. He grabbed Olivia by the hand and pulled her into a vacant office, shutting the door behind them.

"Gabe, I—"

His mouth stopped up her words with a kiss. His hands came up to frame her face as he drove her back against the wall and staked a claim she was willing to answer. "Are you hurt?" He kissed her again. "I don't think I'll ever get used to seeing you in the line of fire like that." She caught his lips and assured him she was in one piece. "I know you're good at what you do. But a little part of me just wants to—"

Olivia kissed him soundly, tangling her fingers in his thick hair, holding him close for a moment before pushing him away to latch on to the lapels of his jacket and rest her hands against his chest. "Did you mean what you said back there? That you love me? We've only known each other a few days. It hasn't exactly been an ideal courtship."

A smile spread across his mouth, softening the chiseled angles of his face and lighting a spark in his handsome blue eyes. "If it's the right person, it doesn't take forever to fall in love."

She answered with a smile that reached deep into her heart. "You are a writer, aren't you? That's a good line."

"I'm a reporter. I tell the truth." He brushed her bangs off her forehead and gently touched his thumb to the skin beside her scraped cheek. "I don't want every week to be like this one—I don't know how many times my heart can handle seeing you get hurt. But being together suits us, don't you think? A couple of workaholics with plenty of emotional baggage. I think we have to dive in to happiness when it finds us."

Olivia nodded. "We both know how rare and fleeting it can be." She slipped her arms around his neck and pressed her body against the solid strength of his. "What about my family? I know they want me to be happy, but getting involved with the man who slammed the department in his newspaper? You're going to take some getting used to."

Gabe's arms settled around her waist. "I don't know. I think your dad and I can agree on one thing."

"What's that?"

"That you are the most special woman in the world—and all we want is for you to be happy and safe."

"You make me happy. And I keep myself safe."

"We'll work on that."

She stretched up on tiptoe and welcomed his kiss. But there was one last ghost between them. "What about you, Gabe? Have you really let Dani go? Is there a place for me in your heart?"

"She'll always be a part of me. But I've said goodbye. Thanks to you, I've finally done right by her—her story will be told and her killer will be in jail." Those piercing blue eyes looked down into hers and she knew his words were the truth. "She took on the world with such gusto that I'd be doing her a disservice if I didn't look to the future and live my life to the fullest. I want you in it. If you need time, if you need me to make peace with your dad, if you need me to not be so stubborn—"

"That's not going to happen." When she laughed, he joined her.

But when he stopped, he pulled her arms from his neck and captured her hands against the steady beat of his heart. "Please give us a chance."

"Promise you'll always be honest with me?"

"Always. Promise not to whack me over the head when I go all caveman on you?"

"Um…" She had to be honest. There was that whole independent spirit and temper of hers to consider. "I can promise to love you. With everything in me."

"I'll take that promise." He leaned down and captured her lips in a kiss that made her believe his word, a kiss that made her wish there was a lock on this door and an endless amount of time to explore all the wonderful ways this man's hands and mouth could make her go weak in the knees.

But that sentimental romancey stuff wasn't who they were. Knowing they would revisit this precious connection when the timing was right, maybe at his condo later that night, Olivia pulled away with a sigh of regret. "I have reports to fill out."

"I have a story to write."

"We'd better go."

With her hand held firmly in his, Gabe led her out the door. When they reached the end of the hallway, her father rose from the chair where he'd been sitting and blocked their path.

For one moment, a nervous breath locked up Olivia's chest.

Thomas Watson's stern paternal eyes looked straight at Gabe, who stood tall beside her. "If you're going to be spending time with my daughter, I'd like to get to know you better, Mr. Knight. We have a family dinner every Sunday afternoon. My dad grills burgers and brats. We watch baseball and root for the Royals when they're playing. It's football and the Chiefs in the fall."

Gabe didn't bat an eye. "I like a good ball game and a burger."

"Good. You can bring the beer." Olivia released the breath she'd been holding and hugged her father when he leaned in to kiss her cheek and whisper, "Don't let this one break your heart."

"He won't, Dad. I trust him."

Chapter Thirteen

Orange was a lousy color on any man. But with Stephen March's thinning hair and pale brown eyes, he looked especially pitiful. Of course, that helplessly doomed look might be more about the handcuffs and leg irons Stephen wore as he sat in the long Fourth Precinct hallway, awaiting transport to the county jail along with other prisoners due for arraignment tomorrow.

Stephen fidgeted in the plastic chair, clawing at his own hands as the host, ignoring the curious glances and outright stares of the others there, sat beside him.

"I'm disappointed in you, Stephen."

"Shut up." Really? This weak-willed addict who'd been saved from certain death on the street, who'd been so desperate to change his fate, thought copping an attitude with the one person who'd helped him the most was the smart way to go? Stephen rocked back and forth in his chair, refusing the guidance and friendship that had been offered so willingly for so long. "You should have let me kill her. Instead, she arrested me."

"Let you?" The host laughed at the absurdity, but spoke in a hushed whisper. "You barely accomplished the task when I sent you to kill Danielle Reese."

"You should have let me kill that detective, and

stopped her from poking around in my business. Then all this would have gone away." Stephen needed a fix so badly that his scratching fingers were drawing blood. "Now I'm going to prison and there's nobody to look after my sister."

Fear had always been an easy motivator—fear of not having any money, not having a home, not being able to afford a dime bag to keep his teeth from rattling out of his head—fear that the one person he'd always been able to count on would be taken from him. But that fear had given way to panic and desperation, two volatile emotions that were much harder to reason with and control.

"That's right, Stephen. You made a mistake, and now you're going to have to pay for it. Perhaps if you had listened to me, if you'd trusted my wisdom and experience, you'd still be a free man. I told you it was a perfect plan. But you strayed from it. I sent my friend to help you escape from the hospital, but once again, you wouldn't do as you were told. You hesitated when he told you to come with him. Now my friend is dead and look where you are." A glance up and down the hallway at the thieves, gangbangers and molesters set to make the same trip were warning enough. "I can make your stay in prison easier for you if you let me."

The chains rattled as Stephen shook his head and scooted to the far side of his chair. "It's not my fault your friend died. I'm not your puppet, anymore. You're not going to talk me into anything else."

True, they would no longer have easy access to each other. And their future meetings would be infrequent if they happened at all. But even through prison bars, there were ways to reach out to Stephen—to use him again if needed, or just to keep an eye on him to ensure his continued cooperation.

"I'm glad we could have this one last talk, then. Good luck. And remember, one word about our agreement, one mention of my name…just think how easy it will be to get to your sister with you stuck on the inside."

"Leave Rosemary alone." Stephen's wide, fearful eyes induced a rush of satisfaction. The rebellion had been brief.

And if, for some reason, Stephen March should grow a backbone and reveal anything more than his role in murdering Danielle Reese, there would be numerous ways, with enough money and the right persuasion, to reach out and silence him.

Permanently.

GABE LOOKED UP from his computer as Olivia walked into his office with two cups of coffee. He smiled. Her eyes were a pale gray-green, meaning she was content. No temper brewing. No overwhelming stress that required a private time-out. Or a shared time-out in a hot, steamy shower that started with a relaxing massage and ended up in the bed with damp sheets and her dozing on his chest.

Now he was really smiling. "So how's my favorite cop?"

She set the coffee on his desk and circled behind his chair. "You promised me lunch. And I believe you have proved yourself to be a man of your word."

Olivia hugged her arms around his shoulders and Gabe turned his head to kiss her.

"So what are you working on?" she asked.

"Making amends." He reached up to squeeze her

hand. "I finished my front-page article for the morning paper. What do you think of the headline, Detective?"

PRAISE FOR KCPD
6 YO MURDER SOLVED/KILLER BEHIND BARS

* * * * *

*The mystery continues in the next
exciting installment of
THE PRECINCT: COLD CASE miniseries
by USA TODAY bestselling author Julie Miller.
Coming in August 2015.
Look for it wherever Harlequin Intrigue books
and ebooks are sold!*

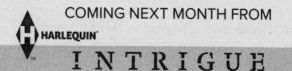
Available April 21, 2015

#1563 SHOWDOWN AT SHADOW JUNCTION
Big "D" Dads: The Daltons • by Joanna Wayne
When Jade Dalton escapes a ruthless kidnapper on the trail of a
multimillion-dollar necklace, Navy SEAL Booker Knox will do whatever
it takes to protect the beautiful event planner. Failure isn't an option.

#1564 TWO SOULS HOLLOW
The Gates • by Paula Graves
Ginny Coltrane might hold the key to proving Anson Daughtry's
innocence. But when Ginny is dragged into a drug war, Anson may be
her only hope of escaping with her life.

#1565 SCENE OF THE CRIME: KILLER COVE
by Carla Cassidy
Accused of murder, Bo McBride has finally returned to Lost Lagoon to
clear his name—with the help of sexy Claire Silver. But as they investigate,
it doesn't take long to realize that danger stalks Claire...

#1566 NAVY SEAL JUSTICE
Covert Cowboys, Inc. • by Elle James
After former Navy SEAL James Monahan and FBI agent Melissa Bradley's
mutual friend goes missing, they join forces to find him. But as a band of
dangerous criminals closes in, survival means trusting each other—their
toughest mission yet.

#1567 COWBOY INCOGNITO
The Brothers of Hastings Ridge Ranch • by Alice Sharpe
A roadtrip to uncover Zane Doe's identity exposes his *real* connection to
Kinsey Frost—and the murderous intentions of those once close to her. Now
Zane must protect her from someone who wants to silence her for good.

#1568 UNDER SUSPICION
Bayou Bonne Chance • by Mallory Kane
Undercover NSA agent Zach Winters vows to solve his best friend's
murder. With the criminals closing in, Zach will risk his own life to protect
a vulnerable widow and her beautiful bodyguard, Madeleine Tierney—the
woman he can't imagine saying goodbye to.

REQUEST YOUR FREE BOOKS!
2 FREE NOVELS PLUS 2 FREE GIFTS!

HARLEQUIN

INTRIGUE

BREATHTAKING ROMANTIC SUSPENSE

YES! Please send me 2 FREE Harlequin Intrigue® novels and my 2 FREE gifts (gifts are worth about $10). After receiving them, if I don't wish to receive any more books, I can return the shipping statement marked "cancel." If I don't cancel, I will receive 6 brand-new novels every month and be billed just $4.74 per book in the U.S. or $5.24 per book in Canada. That's a savings of at least 14% off the cover price! It's quite a bargain! Shipping and handling is just 50¢ per book in the U.S. and 75¢ per book in Canada.* I understand that accepting the 2 free books and gifts places me under no obligation to buy anything. I can always return a shipment and cancel at any time. Even if I never buy another book, the two free books and gifts are mine to keep forever.

182/382 HDN F42N

Name _____ (PLEASE PRINT) _____

Address _____ Apt. # _____

City _____ State/Prov. _____ Zip/Postal Code _____

Signature (if under 18, a parent or guardian must sign) _____

Mail to the **Harlequin® Reader Service:**
IN U.S.A.: P.O. Box 1867, Buffalo, NY 14240-1867
IN CANADA: P.O. Box 609, Fort Erie, Ontario L2A 5X3
Are you a subscriber to Harlequin Intrigue books
and want to receive the larger-print edition?
Call 1-800-873-8635 or visit www.ReaderService.com.

* Terms and prices subject to change without notice. Prices do not include applicable taxes. Sales tax applicable in N.Y. Canadian residents will be charged applicable taxes. Offer not valid in Quebec. This offer is limited to one order per household. Not valid for current subscribers to Harlequin Intrigue books. All orders subject to credit approval. Credit or debit balances in a customer's account(s) may be offset by any other outstanding balance owed by or to the customer. Please allow 4 to 6 weeks for delivery. Offer available while quantities last.

Your Privacy—The Harlequin® Reader Service is committed to protecting your privacy. Our Privacy Policy is available online at www.ReaderService.com or upon request from the Harlequin Reader Service.

We make a portion of our mailing list available to reputable third parties that offer products we believe may interest you. If you prefer that we not exchange your name with third parties, or if you wish to clarify or modify your communication preferences, please visit us at www.ReaderService.com/consumerschoice or write to us at Harlequin Reader Service Preference Service, P.O. Box 9062, Buffalo, NY 14269. Include your complete name and address.

HI13R

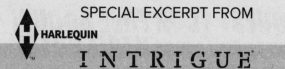

SPECIAL EXCERPT FROM

HARLEQUIN

INTRIGUE

Bo McBride, accused but never arrested for the murder of his girlfriend two years ago, has finally returned to Lost Lagoon, Mississippi, to clear his name with Claire Silber's help. But it doesn't take long for them to realize that real danger stalks Claire.

Read on for a sneak preview of
SCENE OF THE CRIME: KILLER COVE,
the latest crime scene book from
New York Times *bestselling author*
Carla Cassidy.

"So, your turn. Tell me what you've been doing for the last two years," Claire asked. "Have you made yourself a new, happy life? Found a new love? I heard through the grapevine that you're living in Jackson now."

Bo nodded at the same time the sound of rain splattered against the window. "I opened a little bar and grill, Bo's Place, although it's nothing like the original." His dark brows tugged together in a frown, as if remembering the highly successful business he'd had here in town before he was ostracized.

He took another big drink and then continued, "There's no new woman in my life. I don't even have friends. Hell, I'm not even sure what I'm doing here with you."

"You're here because I'm a bossy woman," she replied. She got up to refill his glass. "And I thought you could use an extra friend while you're here."

She handed him the fresh drink and then curled back up

in the corner of the sofa. The rain fell steadily now. She turned on the end table lamp as the room darkened with the storm.

For a few minutes they remained silent. She could tell by his distant stare toward the opposite wall that he was lost inside his head.

Despite his somber expression, she couldn't help but feel a physical attraction to him that she'd never felt before. Still, that wasn't what had driven her to seek contact with him, to invite him into her home. She had an ulterior motive.

A low rumble of thunder seemed to pull him out of his head. He focused on her and offered a small smile of apology. "Sorry about that. I got lost in thoughts of everything I need to get done before I leave town."

"I wanted to talk to you about that," she said.

He raised a dark brow. "About all the things I need to take care of?"

"No, about you leaving town."

"What about it?"

She drew a deep breath, knowing she was putting her nose in business that wasn't her own, and yet unable to stop herself. "Doesn't it bother you knowing that Shelly's murderer is still walking these streets, free as a bird?"

His eyes narrowed slightly. "Why are you so sure I'm innocent?" he asked.

Love the Harlequin book
you just read?

Your opinion matters.

Review this book on your favorite
book site, review site, blog or your own
social media properties and share
your opinion with other readers!

Be sure to connect with us at:
Harlequin.com/Newsletters
Facebook.com/HarlequinBooks
Twitter.com/HarlequinBooks

HARLEQUIN®

A *Romance* FOR EVERY MOOD™

JUST CAN'T GET ENOUGH?

Join our social communities
and talk to us online.

You will have access to the latest
news on upcoming titles and special
promotions, but most importantly,
you can talk to other fans about your
favorite Harlequin reads.

Harlequin.com/Community

 Facebook.com/HarlequinBooks

 Twitter.com/HarlequinBooks

Pinterest.com/HarlequinBooks

THE WORLD IS BETTER WITH

Romance

Harlequin has everything from contemporary, passionate and heartwarming to suspenseful and inspirational stories.

Whatever your mood, we have a romance just for you!

Connect with us to find your next great read, special offers and more.

 /HarlequinBooks

@HarlequinBooks

www.HarlequinBlog.com

www.Harlequin.com/Newsletters

HARLEQUIN®

A *Romance* FOR EVERY MOOD™

www.Harlequin.com